I0762796

NORTH TO DEADWOOD

Also by Wayne D. Overholser and available from Center Point Large Print:

Standoff at the River
Beyond the Pass
Nugget City
Bitter Wind

NORTH TO DEADWOOD

Wayne D. Overholser

CENTER POINT LARGE PRINT
THORNDIKE, MAINE

This Center Point Large Print edition
is published in the year 2026 by arrangement with
Golden West Inc.

The text of this Large Print edition is unabridged.
In other aspects, this book may vary
from the original edition.
Printed in the United States of America
on permanent paper sourced using
environmentally responsible foresting methods.
Set in 16-point Times New Roman type.

ISBN: 979-8-89164-896-8

The Library of Congress has cataloged this record
under Library of Congress Control Number: 2026932479

Chapter 1

Dakota Jones backed up to the cherrywood bar in the Palace saloon, planted his elbows, and looked out over the room crowded with cowboys, miners bound for the Black Hills, and soldiers from Fort D. A. Russell. He wore a .45 in a holster on his right thigh and a knife in a beaded scabbard on his left. He rubbed his big hands over the front of his buckskin shirt and flexed his muscles to loosen them up.

Three days ago, he had ridden into Cheyenne from the Wind River country. Now he was broke, full of bad whisky and ugly temper, and the kind of frustration that could be relieved only by a wing-ding of a fight.

Dakota knew better than most that this year of 1876 was the beginning of the end of the old free days. The military would break the Indian power on the Powder River and in the north, in the Yellowstone country. General Crook was already on his way north from Fort Fetterman with 1,500 men. Miners would pour into the Black Hills and cut down the trees and bore holes into the ground. Then the farmers would come and plow land that never should have been plowed.

Dakota Jones was going to have to change his way of life because his world was changing.

And he didn't like it. He laid his broad-brimmed black hat on the bar and rubbed his hands together.

Behind him, the bartender said, "Don't start it, Jones. I seen you tear this place apart three years running, and that's enough."

Dakota let out a great, challenging whoop and bellowed, "I'm half alligator and half grizzly, and I'm all man. I can lick any four sons of bitches in the place."

No one looked directly at him. Some knew who he was, some didn't, but no one in the saloon wanted any part of him. The bartender glanced at the tall man in the Prince Albert coat who stood at the foot of the stairs just inside the bat wings. He was watching Dakota as if fascinated. The bartender walked quickly to him.

"Sam, hadn't I better stop this before he gets started?"

Sam Hargadine shook his head.

"He's Dakota Jones," the bartender said worriedly. "He spends the winter with the Shoshones, and he gets here in June plumb full of beans. He ain't been in Cheyenne since you bought the place, but I'm warning you—"

"I know who he is," Hargadine said impatiently, "and I want to see if he's half the fighter they say he is."

The bartender moved back to stand behind Dakota. Dakota yelled a few more choice insults, but everyone kept on pretending to be blind and deaf.

Four men were playing poker directly in front of Dakota—three cowboys and one of the Palace gamblers. Dakota stepped forward. He said loudly, "You cowhands are chuckleheaded idiots for playing with that cardsharp. I'm doing you a favor by busting up your game."

He grabbed one corner of the table and flipped it over. Cards and poker chips cascaded to the floor. He moved back and waited expectantly. All four men came up out of their chairs as if by common agreement. They drove at Dakota, who bellowed a great laugh and hit the first man on the jaw with a pile-driving right. The blow lifted him off his feet and knocked him cold.

The remaining three men, two cowboys and the gambler, got in solid blows that had no more effect on Dakota than buzzing horse flies would have in a gelding's ear. He grabbed the gambler and lifted him above his head and threw him halfway across the room. The tinhorn hit the floor just beyond the upset poker table and lay motionless.

The two cowboys stood in front of Dakota, throwing punches to his chest and belly. Dakota grunted as he gave one of them a blow to the side of his head that sent him spinning. Then he said to the one still on his feet, "You're a puny young'un, ain't you?" and hit him in the stomach.

The cowboy's knees turned to rubber, and he bent forward, struggling for breath, his mouth sagging open, his face white.

Dakota rubbed his hands together again and let out another great whoop. "Come on, now!" he roared. "I got to have enough of a fight to work up a sweat. What's the matter with you dudes?"

The bartender had stood it as long as he could. He reached behind the bar, picked up a sawed-off billiard cue, and brought it down across the top of Dakota's head.

Dakota blinked. He turned to look at the bartender.

"Spike," he said slowly, "you oughta be more careful. You could give a man a headache doing a thing like that."

One of the gamblers spoke urgently to Hargadine.

"Sam, he just might kill Spike for that. And the law won't touch him after what Spike done."

Hargadine nodded. "All right. Stop it."

The gambler, Duke Wynne, was only average in height, but big-boned and chunky. He drew his gun as he moved toward Dakota, who had grabbed the bartender and had dragged him over the top of the bar and was shaking him the way a terrier shakes a rat to death. Wynne slammed Dakota across the head with the barrel of his gun. Dakota went to his knees. His eyes turned glassy, and slowly he toppled forward on his face.

The bartender picked himself up, scared and trembling and sweating. Hargadine waved the crowd away.

"The trouble's over," he said. "Go on back to whatever you were doing."

Duke Wynne shook his head. "You're making a mistake, Sam. He's a good man when he ain't drinking, but you get him loaded up on coffin varnish and—"

"I want him," Hargadine said impatiently, and motioned to the Burke twins, who were drinking at the far end of the bar.

"Carry Jones up to my room," he told them. "I'll get Abby."

Duke Wynne put a hand on Hargadine's shoulder. He said, "Sam, you don't know this man. I tell you he ain't the kind of man you want."

Hargadine shook Wynne's hand off his shoulder.

"Get back to your table," he said.

He strode past the Burke twins, who were carrying Dakota's inert body between them, took the stairs three at a time, and walked rapidly around the balcony to a door marked, Abby. He knocked. A moment later, a woman opened the door. She had big blue eyes, and her blonde hair hung down her back in two long braids. She was forty or more, but still a fine-looking, buxom woman.

"You're early," she said. "The water's hot, but I didn't expect you—"

"Come on." He jerked his head impatiently. "I've got a job for you."

She sighed as she shut the door. "Oh, Sam, I'm getting tired of—"

"You're well paid," he said. "Come on."

She followed him back along the balcony to his apartment at the head of the stairs. They went through his parlor and on into his bedroom. The heat from the big range in the kitchen could be felt in the bedroom.

Dakota Jones lay on the bed, breathing hard, a trickle of blood flowing down his forehead. Abby stopped. "Sam, if you've killed—"

"He's alive," Hargadine said. "He's not the kind of a man you can kill by hitting him on the head."

The Burke twins laughed. They were identical except that Jubal had a red scar on his right cheek that had come from a knife gash. They had worked for Hargadine since he had bought the Palace last September, but he still couldn't tell Jubal from Tubal unless he saw the scar.

Abby curled her nose, sniffing audibly. "He smells like an Indian. What do you want me to do with him?"

"Take off that buckskin suit he's wearing," Hargadine said. "Give him a bath. Cut his hair and trim that beard until it looks like a beard instead of a bear rug. And—"

"Oh, no!" Abby began backing toward the door. "I'm willing to cook your meals and patch your clothes and heat water for your bath and sleep with you, but by God, when it comes to cleaning up a monster like this—"

Hargadine had already walked past her. At the door he turned, nodding at the Burke twins.

"Give her a hand, boys. He'll be hurting like hell when he wakes up. He might be mean, but again, he might be sick enough to behave. Jubal, when you get done cleaning him up, go down to Pierre's place and buy him another suit of buckskin."

"What about *your* bath?" Abby demanded.

"Give it to Jones," Hargadine said. "Also, Abby, you'll sleep out here in the other room on the couch. If he wants anything, give it to him. I'll sleep in your bed."

She walked toward him, her hands on her hips, her lips squeezed tightly together. "Sam, what are you up to?"

Hargadine motioned to the unconscious man. "Do you know who he is?"

"Of course I know who he is," Abby said angrily. "Everybody in Cheyenne knows who he is. And when he finds out what's happened to him, he'll kill you."

"No, he won't, Abby."

Hargadine opened the door. “Sam,” Abby cried, “I asked you what you were up to!”

He left the room, making no pretense of answering her. She ran to the door, screaming after him, “Have you still got that crazy notion in your head about going to—” She stopped and heaved a long sigh. “I’m wasting my breath talking to him.”

Alone with Jubal and Tubal, she reached behind her head and drew one of her blonde braids around in front of her eyes. “In another month,” she told the braid, “you’ll be hanging from the lodge pole of some Sioux warrior.”

Jubal and Tubal just grinned. Abby flung the braid over her shoulder.

“Take his buckskins off,” she said, “and stand them in a corner. Then we’ll just keep digging till we reach his own skin.”

Chapter 2

The hours of darkness and early morning were nightmare hours, so filled with a mixture of fantasy and reality that Dakota couldn't distinguish one from the other. He knew he had a thundering headache, but it was the only part of the nightmare that he could tell was real.

It seemed as if he was in a civilized-type bed with brass knobs on top of the corner posts, but that could be part of the dream. He hadn't spent a night in a civilized bed for years. He thought two funny-looking jaspers were floating around the bed, taking off his clothes, but when he tried to fight them, they backed off, and the only thing he managed to do was add to his pounding headache. And then he slid off into darkness again.

Later in the night, he had a mixed-up dream about being carried into another room and dropped into a pool of hot water. Then the dream got wilder than ever, because this here blonde woman came in and began washing him with a sweet-smelling soap of some kind that was the damnedest thing he had ever smelled in his life. And after that, she took a pair of scissors and began snipping at his head. He tried to fight her off, but it didn't work any better than it had with the two men. He couldn't see them anymore, but now his arms were too heavy to lift off the bed. He couldn't even take a good swipe at the woman to drive her away.

A voice said, "He's coming around, Tubal."

And another voice said, "Well, it's about time, Jubal."

Dakota opened his eyes and quickly shut them again.

"Go tell Abby," the first voice said. "She'll cook him up a bit of breakfast, and then we can go to bed."

Dakota sneaked a cautious look. He saw one of the men turn and walk out of the room. The other one continued to stand there and stare down at him. Dakota said, "I don't savvy this. First I see two of you, and then one of you walks off, and now I only see one of you."

The man laughed. "Nothing wrong with your eyes, Dakota. There's two of us. We're the Burke twins. That was Tubal who left." He pointed to the scar on his cheek. "I'm Jubal. This is the way you tell us apart."

Dakota sighed and tenderly touched his head. "What happened? Roof fall in or something?"

Jubal nodded. "Something like that. Better get up and see if you can navigate. Sam Hargadine will be in pretty soon, and he'll want to talk to you."

Dakota sat up and dropped flat again. His skull felt as if it had been parted by a down-sweeping blow of an ax. My God, he thought, it must have been some roof.

"Come on, get up," Jubal said. "You wouldn't want to disappoint Sam, would you?"

"Who the hell is Sam?"

"He's the owner of the Palace."

"Well, I don't know him, and I don't want to talk to him." Dakota sat up again, and this time he gritted his teeth and stayed up until the worst of the pain subsided. "Gimme my pants, and I'll get out of here."

"Can't do that," Jubal said. "Abby, she's the woman who gave you the bath—"

"You mean a woman really did give me a bath?" Dakota said. "Why should a woman give me a bath? You're lying to me!"

Jubal grinned. "Oh, she gave you a bath, all right. She said you shaped up like a lot of man, too."

"Aw, you're joshing me," Dakota said.

"And after the bath," Jubal said, "she took your clothes and burned 'em. They was a mite gamey, you know."

Dakota sat there, taking inventory. He had his drawers on, nothing more. He saw his gunbelt, beaded scabbard, moccasins, and black hat, all tossed on top of a big bureau.

He got to his feet and almost pitched forward on his face. He grabbed the brass knob on top of the nearest bedpost. When the room quit turning, he staggered to the bureau and, gripping the sides, looked at himself in the mirror. He had only about three inches of beard left. It was neatly trimmed along the edges as well as the bottom. Most of his hair was gone, too.

He let out a yell of fury.

"Where is that Delilah?" he demanded.

"Right here, Mr. Jones."

He turned, one hand still clutching the end of the bureau. A blonde woman stood there, her hands on her hips. She was smiling at him, and she was wearing a soft, clinging maroon robe that gave a man the idea that the abundant curves underneath would be right pleasurable to handle.

"I apologize for the bad haircut, Mr. Jones," she said, "although I thought I did a pretty good job with your beard. If you'd care to sit in one of these straight-backed chairs, I can tidy up some of the uneven spots in your hair."

"No, you don't," he said. "You'll never get a pair of scissors on me again if I can help it. Or a razor, either."

The woman shrugged.

"Let bygones be bygones," she said. "Your breakfast is ready, and my name is Abby Carter. I expect we'll be seeing quite a bit of each other from now on."

"Why?"

"Because I'm a kind of companion and general flunky for Sam Hargadine." She motioned to him. "Come on and eat your breakfast."

He followed her into the kitchen, sat down at the table, and picked up the cup of steaming coffee she had poured for him. Jubal followed. The other twin was standing beside the range, holding a cup of coffee in his hand.

Abby brought him a plate of bacon and eggs, another plate with flapjacks, and a pitcher of syrup. She filled his coffee cup and took the pot back to the stove. He ate wolfishly, and his headache faded. He pushed the plates back and drank the rest of the coffee.

"Who dropped that knockout pill into my last drink?" he asked Abby. "Did you do that, too? You seem capable of doing a lot of things."

"Oh, I am, Mr. Jones, I am," Abby said, "but I didn't do that."

She disappeared into the bedroom. Jubal said, "You didn't get no knockout pill, Dakota. You cleaned out a poker game, and then Spike tried to put you down by hitting you on the head with a sawed-off billiard cue. But you turned around and hauled him over the bar and just about shook his teeth out of his head—"

"I remember that," Dakota said. "But it's the last thing I *do* remember."

"Duke Wynne figured you were going to kill Spike, so he cracked you across the noggin with his gun barrel. That's what put you down."

"Who's Duke Wynne?"

"One of Hargadine's dealers."

"A tinhorn," Dakota groaned. "I hate tinhorns. I'll kill the bastard."

Jubal laughed. "He took the train to Sidney early this morning. You won't see him for a while."

Abby returned with a box of cigars. "I found these in the living room, Mr. Jones. You might just as well have one. You twins, too. We don't get a chance to take over the great man's apartment very often, so we'd better make ourselves at home."

Dakota picked up a cigar and sniffed at it.

"It don't smell much," he said. "Not like a cigar ought to."

"It's a good Havana," Tubal said, "the best Hargadine can buy. Sam Hargadine always travels first class."

Dakota took the match that Abby handed him and fired the cigar. He leaned back in his chair, staring thoughtfully at the Burke twins. They were in their early twenties, he judged. They wore range clothes and cowboy boots; their faces were tanned to a leathery brown except for narrow white strips along their foreheads that were protected from the sun by their Stetsons.

"What does this fellow Hargadine want with me?" Dakota asked. "Seems like he went to a lot of trouble on my account."

"He did for a fact," Abby said, "but he'll have to tell you himself. I laid out your new buckskin outfit, by the way. He had Jubal get it for you last night."

"A lot of trouble," Dakota said, "and a lot of money to boot. What do you people do for Hargadine?"

The Burke twins exchanged glances; then Jubal said, "It's like Abby told you. We're general flunkies."

"Bodyguards," Tubal added. "Bouncers. Messengers. Any damn thing Sam needs done."

"The three of us have one thing to offer that the others who stuck around Sam don't have," Abby said. "Call it loyalty if you want to. We wouldn't sell him out. That's what it boils down to."

"Funny thing about Sam," Jubal said. "He's smart, and he's tough, but there's times when somebody's got to take care of him."

Abby nodded. "That's sure the truth."

"I'll go get my clothes," Dakota said, "and put 'em on."

"It's time you got dressed," Abby said. "Sam will be along any time."

"I ain't waiting for him," Dakota said. "I'm getting the hell out of here. I picked up a haircut, a beard trim, a bath, breakfast, and a new suit of buckskin. I didn't ask for any of those things, but I got 'em anyway. Now I'm getting out before I pick up a few more things I don't want."

The Burke boys shook their heads.

"You're talking to Sam first," Tubal said.

The Burkes were about as tall as Dakota and nearly as heavy. If Dakota didn't have a skulling to get over, he probably could take both of them, but right then, he had no desire to try. Secretly, he was curious about Sam Hargadine.

"All right," he said, "I'll talk to your Hargadine, and then I'll pull my freight."

Abby laughed. "No, you won't, Mr. Jones. Sam's a magician. After you talk to him, you'll decide you don't want to."

Chapter 3

Dakota sat in Sam Hargadine's parlor, wearing the new buckskin suit. He felt as uncomfortable as a small boy dressed up for church and wearing tight button shoes.

"It don't feel right," he complained to Abby, "and it don't smell right either. When I get out of this damn town, I'll kill me a buffler and gut him and roll in the guts. That'll change the smell in a hurry."

She gave him a sharp look, not certain whether he was joshing or not. She said, "I don't understand you, Mr. Jones. You're two men, seems like."

He looked down at the half-smoked cigar in his hand, knowing exactly what she meant. He had been aware that he was two men from the time he had ridden out of Black Hawk, Colorado, years ago, and, drifting north, had adopted the free life of a mountain man.

He had often wondered about Kit Carson and Jim Bridger and the others, men who had been raised in the East. Did they ever entirely discard the training of those early years, the teachings that had been dinned into them during their boyhood?

He didn't know about them, but he did know

about himself. He would never entirely free himself from all of the attitudes his mother had given him; he could never fully enjoy the amoral life of a man who lives with the Indians, refusing all responsibility and never staying in one place long enough to let his roots go down.

Dakota had not been satisfied with his life, and now at thirty, he knew he was going to change it. He wasn't sure how, though. He wasn't sure he could stand the discipline of a steady job, the nagging and criticism of a boss who had never known what it was to be a free man. The more he thought about it, the more worried he got.

He put the cigar back into his mouth and chewed on it a moment. "All right," he said, "I'm two men. Are you only one woman?"

She had been standing by a window looking down into the street. She said, "I'd better go change the bed before the great man comes in," and started across the room.

"You didn't answer my question," Dakota said.

She stopped beside him, shaking her head. "I shouldn't have said what I did. I didn't realize I was hitting a raw nerve with you. But I'll tell you straight out—you sure as hell hit one with me."

She was, he thought, a kind and decent woman, and he liked her.

"The notion came to me just now that maybe we've got the same problem," he said. "I've had mine for quite a spell, and coming to town once a year and getting drunk and having a fight and getting slammed over the head with a gun barrel don't change anything."

"And what is your problem?"

He shrugged. "Just being two men, I guess. I was sixteen when my mother died. There wasn't anything to hold me, so I rode out of town and kept on riding. I've lived with the Sioux and the Shoshones, and I've learned to do things that not many white men can do, but I ain't satisfied. I try not to think about it, but some of the things my ma taught me are still in my head. That's where the two men come in. By the time you're sixteen, a lot of notions have got stuck in your thinking. I've lived a free life, but I've never got 'em all out of my noggin."

"That's the way I had it figured with you," she said. "It's not quite the same with me. My ma never taught me a damn thing except that I'd better take care of myself 'cause nobody else was going to. I'm two women, all right. I'm a whore and a housekeeper. Nobody else wants to take over the housekeeping, but when it comes to the whoring part, there's a young redhead named Janie who's trying to push me out of Sam's bed. By God, I'll kill her before I let her do it."

Abby whirled and ran out of the room as the hall door opened. Sam Hargadine came in. Dakota remembered seeing him in the Palace, although he hadn't known who he was. Tall, slender, handsome, immaculately dressed, Hargadine outwardly was the typical gambler who could win or lose everything on the turn of a card, without once betraying excitement.

Still, Dakota sensed something about the man that set him apart from other gamblers he had known. For one thing, Hargadine's smile was quick and warm as he held out his hand and moved toward Dakota.

"I'm glad to see you up and around, Jones. Last night I wasn't sure you would make it by noon today."

"I feel fine except for a headache," Dakota said mildly.

Hargadine's grip was strong, his dark eyes met Dakota's squarely. He turned toward the sideboard, saying, "Sit down, Jones. I'll pour us a drink. I want a talk with you, a straight talk, because I'm going to hire you. I'll lay the whole deal out in the open so we'll understand each other all the way."

Dakota had been pretty sure that Hargadine had some kind of job offer in mind, and the last thing he wanted to do was work for a gambler. He had been prepared to say no in a tone Hargadine would understand and then walk out. But he didn't. He sat there, took the shot glass from Hargadine, and he smiled as the man said, "Here's to our future association. May it be pleasant and profitable for both of us."

Dakota rolled the bourbon around in the pouch of his cheek and then swallowed it. Good whisky was like good cigars, he decided, and accepted a fresh Havana from the box Hargadine offered. Hargadine selected one, set the box back on the sideboard, and then sank comfortably into a black leather chair.

"Well, you're a good-looking man," Hargadine said. "I couldn't tell much about you last night. That's why I asked Abby to clean you up."

Something about the way he said it made Dakota mad. This Hargadine was an interesting fellow who lived a real stylish life, but he took liberties with people.

"I liked me the way I was," he said. "I didn't ask nobody to clean me up."

Dakota started toward the hall door. Hargadine said pleasantly, "I wouldn't advise you to go through that door, Jones."

Dakota stopped.

"You've got one of your gunslicks out there waiting to smoke me down, huh? Is that it?"

Hargadine shrugged. "All I'm asking is for you to stay until I finish what I have to say. Fair enough?"

Dakota scratched an ear. Hargadine was still smiling pleasantly at him.

"All right," he said, and returned to his chair and chewed on his cigar.

"Good," Hargadine said approvingly. "We're

going to get along fine. First, I'd like to know a little more about you. It's in my mind to offer you a lot of money for your services for a short time, and I'd like to know for sure that you're the kind of man who can deliver the goods."

"If I don't deliver, I don't take money," Dakota said.

"I would expect that," Hargadine said, "from a man who has become a living legend."

"Legend?" Dakota said. "I'm not any legend."

"Oh, come now," Hargadine said. "All men like you are legends long before they cash in their chips. You come to town once a year. You go on a gigantic spree and wreck saloons and flatten anybody who gets in your way. Last night I saw you put four men out of action without mussing your hair. The point is, Jones, I want to give you a very tough job, but it will take more than a fighting man to do it."

Dakota tapped the long, firm ash off his cigar. He still had half a mind to walk out. He could pick Hargadine up by the shoulders and use him as a shield and make it down to the street alive. On the other hand, he *was* interested in money.

He had never seen much money, come right down to it. He sold some pelts in the spring, and at times he came to Cheyenne with a few ponies to sell, and on occasion he had guided hunting parties or a cavalry expedition against the Indians, but he had never really got his paws on more than one hundred dollars at a time.

If whisky didn't take his money, the gamblers did. But it would be nice, just for once, to feel downright rich. He let a big cloud of smoke collect around his palate, and then he blew it out, mellow and rich.

"I was born in Ohio," he said. "I was an only child. My folks were fifty-niners. We moved to Denver when I was thirteen, then we went to Black Hawk, where my father got a job in a mine. He was killed when a tunnel caved in. My mother taught school there until she died in '62. I was sixteen when I rode north into Wyoming. I've been riding ever since, wintering with the Indians—"

"Good," Hargadine said. "You know Indians."

"Nobody knows Indians any more than you can say you know a woman," Dakota said. "I've lived with them, and I like them and admire them in some ways. I reckon you could say I know them about as well as I know white men."

"That's good enough for me," Hargadine said, "but I've heard some things about you that you didn't mention. For instance, you were with the Custer party that went into the Black Hills two years ago, weren't you?"

Dakota stared out of the window. He wasn't proud of having been with Custer, but there was no point in denying it.

"I was with him," he said.

"Is there really gold in the Black Hills?" Hargadine asked. "I mean, a lot of gold that will make a lot of men rich? Or is it a case of a little gold being blown up just to make a few merchants and freighters rich?"

"There's plenty of gold in the Black Hills," Dakota said, "although why you or any other white man has any claim to it is more'n I can understand."

"Well, sir, that's not my worry," Hargadine said. "There's some pretty tall tales told about you, Jones. Like guiding that Englishman, Sir Cedric something or other, into the Powder River country and getting hit by a Cheyenne war party and then bringing old Cedric out alive. And the time the Sioux caught you with some miners on Crazy Woman Creek, and you brought them to Fort Fetterman and lost only one man. These stories true?"

Dakota yawned. "All lies," he said.

Hargadine laughed. "I thought you'd say that. Well, I happen to believe them."

He rose and crossed the room to a wall safe and took out a buckskin sack, letting Dakota hear the *chink* of gold coins. He tossed it to the marble-topped table in the middle of the room.

"I plan to take a wagon train through to the Black Hills," Hargadine said. "I've got good wagons and good mules, and I'm taking some extra animals along. I expect to start a saloon in Deadwood, so I'm taking what I need—whisky, tables, chairs, a bar, everything I'll use to run a saloon. Also, enough supplies to get us to Deadwood and keep us eating for a few weeks after we get there. Now, barring something that can't be foreseen, how long will it take?"

"Depends on the weather," Dakota said. "You might make it in two weeks if everything goes just right, but chances are it'll take longer."

"I want you to guide us," Hargadine said. "I know it's dangerous. If the Indians get wind of the whisky I'm taking, they'll give us hell, so I'm hoping they won't hear about it. Anyhow, it's worth the thousand dollars in that sack yonder for you to guide us up there."

Dakota blinked and swallowed.

With that much money, he could start a small cattle ranch. Be his own boss; set his own hours; make his own deals; and never have to take any lip from another man.

Then he shook his head.

"You're out of your mind, Hargadine. You don't need a guide, let alone pay me that kind of dinero. All you've got to do is follow the road. People are going to the Black Hills all the time."

"It's not that easy," Hargadine said. "Let's just say I'd feel better to know you were out there in front. If you're interested, ride out to Horner's Flat, where my wagons are. You'll find five other wagons that are going along. They may slow us up, but speed isn't important enough to turn them down."

Dakota nodded. "When do you figure to start?"

"In the morning," Hargadine said. "Anyway, look my outfit over. Talk to the people, Jack Rawls in particular. He's my wagon boss, but he'll take your orders on anything that involves safety. I'll be out there later this afternoon and see if you're sure you want to take my offer. I'll tell you again that it's going to be dangerous. I won't feel easy until we pull into Deadwood."

"Uh-huh," Dakota said. "Well, now I'd like to walk through that door without getting my head shot off."

"Why, certainly," Hargadine said.

He opened the door and called to someone in the saloon below. As Dakota crossed the room, he glanced at Abby. She eked out a thin smile, which told him nothing. He winked at her and slouched out.

Chapter 4

Dakota ambled over to the livery stable. He saddled his sorrel gelding, shoved his Winchester in the boot, and rode out of town.

When he reached Horner's Flat, he saw fifteen or more wagons scattered around. The teamsters were busy, getting ready to move in the morning. Five other men were playing cards on blankets that had been spread under some cottonwoods.

Dakota reined up and studied the cardplayers. They glanced at him, then went on playing. Hardcases, he thought. Each carried a six-shooter on his hip, and five Winchesters were leaning against the wagons or the trunks of the cottonwoods. Dakota didn't know any of them, but one or all could be road agents.

No one could identify an outlaw just by looking at him. That was where the shoe pinched and why the outlaws ran free the way they did. They'd hole up with a respectable rancher, or appear to run a small spread or business, and ride the owlhoot on the side. No lawman could be sure who they were, and an employer like Hargadine just had to take his chances. The Sioux and the Cheyenne figured to be out around the Bighorn or the Tongue or the Powder, watching Crook and Terry. These birds could be the real danger.

Dakota rode to the nearest wagon and said, "Where'll I find Jack Rawls?"

The teamster had been greasing an axle. He straightened, then jerked his hand toward a tall man who was talking to another teamster.

"That's him over there."

"Thanks."

Dakota rode to Rawls and dismounted. When the man swung around, Dakota held out his hand.

"I'm Dakota Jones," he said.

The man's face darkened. His eyes narrowed, and his lips thinned, turning down at the corners. He shook Dakota's hand briefly and dropped it and stepped back.

"All right, Jones. Go ahead and talk."

"Sam Hargadine offered me the job of guiding—"

"I heard all about it," Rawls said. "He offered you a hell of a lot of money to guide this outfit over a well-marked road that's got folks going over it every day. I've worked for him for three months buying wagons and mules and saddle horses and hiring teamsters." Rawls motioned toward the men playing cards. "Guards, too. I've put an outfit together that can stand off Indians or road agents or any other damn thing that comes along—but he never made me no offer like he done you."

Dakota knew jealousy when he saw it. Sometimes it was a good idea to pretend it wasn't there.

"I don't aim to interfere with the way you handle the wagons," he said easily, "but I do aim to pick the route and decide where we'll camp and how many guards we'll put out. In other words, you take care of the actual mile-by-mile travel, and I'll work on the safety part of the trip."

Rawls took a plug of tobacco out of his shirt pocket, gnawed off a chew, and slipped the plug back into his pocket. He said, his mouth curling in contempt, "I guess you know about the Indians. You're a man of the country, ain't you, Jones?"

"Man of the country" was a local term for a squaw man. There were any number of them scattered through eastern Wyoming, men who had come in years ago, taken Indian wives, and thrown up crude cabins. Usually, they ran a few cows and hauled wood and hay for the forts or lived by hunting and fishing. And usually they had a flock of half-breed children.

Now, many of them were sending their Indian wives back to the reservation because Wyoming was becoming civilized, and they wanted to attain an acceptable social position. Some were looking for white women to marry.

Anybody who called you a squaw man was hoping to work up a fight. A fight with Rawls was bound to come somewhere on the way to the Black Hills, but there would be better days for it later on.

"No, I'm not a man of the country," Dakota said. "Are the wagons loaded?"

Rawls nodded. "Sam figures to pull out in the morning, but I don't know how far he'll go." He motioned toward five wagons off to the east. "There's the hitch. Them people ain't part of Sam's outfit. They just moved in, and Sam agreed to let 'em go along 'cause he's too softhearted to say no. They're the ones who'll make trouble for us. They won't keep up. They don't have extra horses. They'll break down, and we'll be stuck halfway to Deadwood because Sam won't go off and leave 'em."

"I'll go over and meet 'em," Dakota said.

He walked away, leading his sorrel. The first two wagons were close together. As he came up, he saw two men lying in the grass on the shady side of the near wagon. Two women and several children were sitting or lying in the shade of the far wagon. The ashes of a small fire lay between the wagons, so Dakota guessed the families had been cooking together.

The men had been talking, but they fell silent as Dakota approached them. He said, "I'm Dakota Jones. I'm going to be guiding this wagon train."

"I'm Ira Starbuck," the first man said. "Glad to know you, Jones. Sure heard plenty about you."

"Len Akers," the second man said. "I've heard of you, too. I'm glad we're in good hands."

Dakota moved on, wishing people wouldn't talk like that.

The next wagon belonged to a little man named Bruce Bascom, who had an apologetic air and the sallow expression of one who wasn't in good health. He said, "Mr. Jones, I'm glad you're guiding this train. I don't trust Jack Rawls and those apes he hired."

"Apes?"

"Well, maybe it would be better to call them wolves," Bascom said. "I've done some trading on the Ute reservation in Colorado, and I know the two who call themselves Laird and Summers. Laird's the skinny one. Summers is the big man with the red beard. They've smuggled whisky onto the reservation. I don't trust men like that."

"Neither do I," Dakota said. He wondered if Hargadine knew about Laird and Summers and if it would make any difference if he did.

Bascom raised his voice. "Honey Doll, come here and meet Mr. Dakota Jones."

Dakota had glimpsed a woman hunkered over a small fire on the other side of the wagon, but he had paid no attention to her. He paid attention now though. Mrs. Bascom was the biggest woman he had ever seen in his life. She was taller than Dakota, big-shouldered, broad of beam, and yet she was not out of proportion. She gave the impression of great strength, yet she still contrived to appear feminine. That, Dakota told himself, was quite a trick.

Mrs. Bascom shook hands powerfully, her eyes thoughtful as if she wondered whether she could whip him. She said, "I'm real happy to have you along, Mr. Jones. If we can do anything for you, just sing out."

"Thank you, Mrs. Bascom."

"And if you can do anything for us, Hercules and me will appreciate it."

She turned and walked back to the fire. Her husband said gravely, "What she means, Mr. Jones, is that Rawls doesn't want us to go. We plan to start a store somewhere in the Black Hills, and we have a heavy wagon. Our team is not the best, and Rawls claims we'll slow the train up. But Mr. Hargadine has promised to loan us a team of mules if our horses can't make it."

"And you want me to keep Rawls from throwing you out of the train?"

"That's about it, Mr. Jones." Bascom was embarrassed. He dug a boot toe into the dirt, his gaze on the ground. "I know I'm a mangy little runt, but Honey Doll—well, I tell you, Mr. Jones, she can do anything."

Dakota grinned at him. "I'll see what I can do," he said.

He turned toward the fourth wagon, then stopped. Sam Hargadine had just ridden in on a black gelding. A fine-looking animal, Dakota thought, with a star on his forehead and four white stockings. You could expect Hargadine to ride just such an animal, fast and showy.

Hargadine spoke briefly to Rawls, then wheeled his horse and galloped to where Dakota stood.

"Heard the news, Dakota?"

"What news?"

"Word just reached town that Crook met up with Crazy Horse on the Rosebud. Crazy Horse had a big bunch of Indians and Crook got whipped. At least he pulled back to Goose Creek and he's calling for reinforcements and more ammunition. What does that mean for us?"

"Just what you'd expect," Dakota said. "The Indians will break up into small bands and we're dead sure to run into some of 'em before we get to the Black Hills."

"You think we'd better wait? Or maybe call the trip off?"

"You're the boss," Dakota said, "so it's up to you. As far as I'm concerned, nothing has changed. We'll probably have to fight, but I think we can get through."

He saw the corner of Hargadine's mouth twitch slightly, then relax. The bland expanse of the gambler's face did not otherwise move. Finally Hargadine said, "All right, we'll go ahead."

Chapter 5

A boy stood beside the fourth wagon, watching Dakota stride toward him. He was in his late teens, freckle-faced and tow-headed, with the long-legged look of one who has sprouted up overnight out of his cowhide boots.

"I'm Dakota Jones," Dakota said. "Sam Hargadine hired me to—"

"I know," the boy said. "Jack Rawls told me. I'm Bud Nelson. This wagon belongs to my sister Nora. I'll be driving for her. She's around here cooking supper."

Dakota followed Bud to the back of the wagon, where a young woman was bending over a cook fire.

"Sis, this is Dakota Jones."

She wasn't much older than Bud, maybe twenty, Dakota guessed. She was tall and strong, her face tanned by the sun so that her blue eyes seemed even brighter than they were. Her hair seemed more red than brown. Auburn, he decided. She was, he thought, a real pretty girl.

She smiled and held out her hand.

"I'm Nora Nelson. I'm planning to start a millinery shop in Deadwood unless something better comes along." The smile faded and she added, "We have a good wagon, a light load, and a strong team. We also have a saddle horse. We'll keep up."

"Good," Dakota said. "Then I won't worry about you folks."

He started to walk away, but Bud asked eagerly, "Is it true that you killed a grizzly with your bare hands?"

"Yeah," Dakota said. "It was a day-old sucklin' cub."

This time Bud let him go. When he reached the fifth wagon, he said, "I'm Dakota Jones, and I've been hired to guide this outfit to Deadwood, and if you ask me about any damn lies that keep following me around, I'll skin you all the way from the top of your head to the tip of your tail."

The man was very tall and very thin. He had a drooping yellow mustache. He was smoking a blackened briar pipe, which he took out of his mouth in order to enjoy a good, quiet laugh.

"I'm Barney Ryan," he said. "I'm a teacher hoping to start a school in Deadwood." He paused, gray eyes direct and friendly. "I'm not much of a cook, but I would be honored if you would have supper with me."

Dakota didn't understand it, but he had a funny feeling that he had known Barney Ryan for years, liking and trusting him all the while.

"Glad to," he said. "I don't know what Hargadine meant for me to do about my meals, but it's nothing to him if I eat with you."

Ryan nodded at one of the wagons. "That's the supply wagon. The driver is the cook. He feeds the teamsters and the guards and Rawls. Hargadine probably meant for you to eat with them, but I don't think you would enjoy their company. The teamsters are all right, but Rawls and the guards are a hard bunch."

"I figured they was," Dakota said.

"I'm not sure yet what Rawls is up to," Ryan said, "but he's been telling around that you're a savage and a squaw man, which is none of our business either way."

Dakota shrugged. "I'm used to having all kinds of lies told about me, but it seems purty damn plain to me that Rawls is playing his game and it ain't Hargadine's."

Ryan knocked his pipe out against his heel and slipped it into his pocket. "Everybody sees it but Hargadine. The trouble is, he's out of his element. He's done his share of shearing the lambs, but now it's his turn to get sheared if he doesn't figure things out in a hurry." Ryan sighed. "Well now, I'll slice up a little more side meat, and I hope you'll eat with me all the way to Deadwood."

"Thanks," Dakota said and added thoughtfully, "I get the notion that none of you on this side of the camp trusts Rawls."

"We don't for a fact," Ryan agreed.

"Why don't you pull out and make your own

wagon train? There's plenty of travel on the Black Hills road these days."

"Two reasons," Ryan said. "One is that none of us is very brave. There's plenty of travel on the road and there's also plenty of people getting killed. The other is that we made a bargain with Hargadine. Rawls wants us out of the train for reasons of his own, I guess, but we don't cotton to being bluffed out by that bastard."

"Good enough reasons," Dakota said. "Who is he?"

"None of us knows, but I'll tell you one thing, Mr. Jones. We're glad you're here. We don't know anything about Rawls, but we do know your reputation."

"Hell, friend, most of my reputation is a bunch of lies."

Ryan chuckled. "Well, we figure that even if you didn't do all the great things they say you did, you must have done *something* to get the lies started."

"I'll pull the saddle off my horse and stake him out," Dakota said abruptly.

When he returned to the fire a few minutes later, he saw a covered wagon coming in from Cheyenne. One of the Burke twins was driving. Behind the wagon came a surrey, the other twin handling the lines. Three women were in the surrey. One was Abby. Dakota had never seen the other two before.

"My God," Ryan breathed. "Three of Hargadine's whores. That's just what we need in this train."

Dakota knew Ryan was right, but he just nodded and fell to eating. A little later Jubal came to their fire. Jubal motioned toward a tent that he and Tubal had just put up.

"Sam wants everybody to come to the tent. He's got something to say to all of you."

Jubal wheeled and strode away. Dakota said, "I'll tell you for sure now. Your five wagons would be better off traveling by yourselves."

Ryan shook his head. "The Bascoms will never make it to Deadwood with that heavy wagon and their worn-out team. Hargadine has promised them help." He sighed heavily. "We've been camped here several days waiting to roll. Rawls has wanted to get rid of us, and he's been stinky mean, but we're going to stick together come hell or high water."

Dakota understood. Once they reached the Black Hills, the people in the five wagons would scatter and probably never see each other again, but for the time being, Rawls's open enmity had forced them into an alliance. Also, they accepted Dakota mainly because Rawls opposed him.

Abby stood in front of the tent, two scarlet sisters behind her. One was a small, trim, red-haired girl. The other woman was a blowsy blonde, perhaps not so old as Abby, but close.

Hargadine stood a few feet from Abby, a tall, handsome man, as immaculate as he had been that morning in his office over the Palace saloon. Dakota wondered if he would arrive in Deadwood in the same condition.

"First, I want to assure you that we are taking all the precautions that we can for your safety," Hargadine said. "Jack Rawls will line up the order of march in the morning. Five of my wagons will be in front and five behind." He bowed slightly toward the men who stood grouped around Dakota. "Your wagons will be sandwiched between mine for your greater protection. We will not tolerate any gaps in the line. We do not intend to run our horses to Deadwood, but we won't dawdle, either."

He turned toward Rawls and the guards.

"These men will ride as flankers. Dakota Jones will operate as an outrider. He will scout as far ahead as he feels he should. However, in spite of our precautions, we face danger from the Indians due to Crook's defeat. There is also danger from outlaws. If any of you want to pull out, this is the time."

No one said anything, so Hargadine nodded as if the matter was settled. "We'll be rolling by sunup. If you haven't had your breakfast by then, you'll go hungry. One more thing. None of you will leave the train unless you have permission from Dakota Jones or me. That is all."

Several started to walk away. Then Abby said, "You forgot something, Sam." Smiling devilishly, she motioned toward the covered wagon on the other side of the tent. "The joy wagon is open for business, gentlemen. Janie and Sweet Betsy will be happy to receive you, each and every evening."

Dakota heard gasps from the women around him. Mrs. Bascom actually doubled her huge fists and started toward Abby. Her husband grabbed her arm and hung on like a little bulldog. "Don't lose your temper, Honey Doll. She ain't worth it."

Mrs. Bascom stopped, quivering with anger. She said, her voice shaky, "So help me, I'll clean her plow before we get to Deadwood."

Abby smiled contemptuously. She flounced into the tent, Janie and Sweet Betsy a step behind her. Dakota started toward Ryan's wagon, and then he heard Hargadine's voice.

"Jones, I want to see you."

Dakota sighed, thinking he didn't want to see Hargadine. If he did, he'd be tempted to tell the man he would be starting out in the morning with more potential trouble than a smart man would allow, but that would be a sure way to lose a thousand dollars.

"I'll be along," he said to Ryan and turned back.

Hargadine was talking to Rawls. Everyone else had left except the Burke twins.

"I keep *telling* you," Rawls was saying, "you've *got* to get rid of the Bascoms. They'll never make it to Fort Laramie, let alone Deadwood."

Hargadine swallowed audibly. In the near darkness, Dakota sensed that the man was fighting his temper. Hargadine didn't want a row with his wagon boss, but he'd just about reached the end of his rope. He said, "Jack, you know we have extra mules. If the Bascoms can't keep up, I'll let them have a team."

"That little runt can't handle mules," Rawls said. "The whole business of taking them extra wagons is crazy. Leave 'em here, Sam."

Hargadine threw out a hand in a violent gesture. "I pay the bills, Jack. I give the orders. If you don't like the way things stack up, I'll give you an extra month's wages and you can climb onto your horse and git."

For a moment, Rawls stood his ground, glaring at Hargadine. Then, without a word, he wheeled and strode away into the gathering darkness.

For more than a minute, Hargadine didn't move or speak. He stood motionless, staring after Rawls. He was breathing hard, and Dakota, watching him, sensed that he was not a violent man by nature. He regretted letting his temper get the best of him.

Finally, Hargadine said, "I won't change my mind now, but I wanted to know what you thought about letting these five wagons go with us."

"I figure you've got a reason for taking them," Dakota said.

"I have, damn it. I want to give the impression of a family wagon train. We won't hide the women inside the wagons. The kids will be walking in plain sight. I figure we're less likely to be attacked than if we're an all-man freight outfit, maybe carrying something the outlaws might want."

"Like what?"

Hargadine hesitated. Then he said, "Whisky."

"Your reason is a good one," Dakota said. "It don't apply to Indians, but outlaws know what killing a batch of women and kids would do. Every man in Cheyenne would be after 'em as soon as the news got out."

Hargadine took a long breath. He nodded, mostly to himself. He said, "That's all, Jones."

Later, with his head on his saddle, Dakota stared at the sky with its myriad of twinkling stars and wondered what was really worrying Hargadine. Some way, somehow, Dakota had to find out.

He dropped off—and suddenly the light of dawn had taken over the western sky, and he heard Rawls's great voice, "Roll out! Roll out!"

Within a matter of minutes, cook fires crackled, columns of smoke rose into the thin, chill air, and horses and mules were being watered and fed.

Dakota sipped a cup of Barney Ryan's black,

steaming coffee and did a little thinking. Two nights before, he had been standing at the bar in the Palace saloon without a real care in the world. All he had needed was a little fight. Now he had the lives of a bunch of women and children in his hands.

This was the day Sam Hargadine had been waiting for—the day his wagon train rolled north toward the Black Hills and a big fat fortune. But Sam Hargadine wasn't going to be much help to Dakota Jones. That thousand dollars figured to be pretty tough to earn, after all.

Chapter 6

Dakota saddled his sorrel, helped Barney Ryan harness his team and hook up to the wagon, then mounted and trotted to where Jack Rawls sat his saddle. Dakota said, "We'll camp tonight on Pole Creek."

Rawls gave Dakota a half-inch nod.

Dakota rode on north, smiling a little. He reined up atop a small rise north of camp, hipped around in the saddle, and watched the wagons line out. The sun now showed a bright arc above the eastern horizon. Sam Hargadine rode his black gelding in front as if he were the commander. The surrey came next, and the wagon with the tent and the women's supplies was directly behind the surrey. Hargadine's women would not have to eat any dust.

Five of Hargadine's wagons followed; then the five wagons that didn't belong to Hargadine, with Bascom's the last; and finally the remainder of the Hargadine wagons. The guards had swung out on both sides as flankers, Rawls on the left and slightly in front, the big, red-bearded Summers on the right and about the same distance in front.

Dakota rode north toward Fort Laramie, convinced the train would have no trouble this close to Cheyenne. Probably not tomorrow, either, but after that, anything could happen. Now that

Crook had been thrown back on the Rosebud, small, fast-moving bands of young Cheyenne and Sioux warriors would sweep across the Wyoming plains looking for horses and cheap scalps.

Twice later in the day, Dakota stopped on the crests of long swells and looked back at the line of wagons, swaying and dipping like full-rigged ships in this rolling sea of grass. He admitted to himself that Rawls knew his business, halting on the long slopes to rest the horses.

Right from the start, it was clear that Rawls's judgment of the Bascom wagon was correct. The first time Dakota stopped, a gap showed in front of the Bascoms. The second time, Hargadine's five rear wagons had passed the Bascoms, and the gap was wider than ever.

Dakota made a wide swing west of the road toward the Laramie range. As a matter of principle, he poked into every grove of cottonwoods and nest of willows that he saw. He made an equally careful study of the moist valley bottoms as he crossed them.

Several times he noticed mounted men riding fast on the Fort Laramie road to the east. He guessed they were Black Hillers, discounting Indian danger and determined to reach the gold fields ahead of the rush. They were prime prospects for losing their scalps.

He reached Pole Creek ahead of the wagon train. Dismounting, he loosened the cinch and watered his horse, then lay on the grass and stared at the clouds that were being driven eastward by the wind. For some reason, the girl, Nora Nelson, slipped into his mind and stayed there awhile. Then he laughed at himself. He had never seen her until yesterday afternoon. He had exchanged maybe a dozen words with her, and here he was, dreaming about her like a schoolboy. Still, he liked her honest, straightforward way of talking. Most white women now, they acted like they were going to say yes and then ended up saying no . . .

He saw Hargadine and the surrey break over the ridgetop to the south. He rose, tightened the cinch, and rode up the slope to meet them. By the time he reached Hargadine, the entire train—except for the Bascom wagon—was rolling down-grade.

Dakota reined in beside Hargadine. "Where's the Bascoms?"

Hargadine shrugged. "Coming, I guess. I'll see they get a team of mules in the morning."

Dakota nodded. "I'll take a sashay back along the trail and see where they are." He rode up the slope. Abby smiled and waved to him as he passed the surrey.

When he reached the Nelson wagon, he saw that Bud was driving, with Nora beside him on the seat. Their saddle horse, a bay gelding, was tied behind the wagon. Dakota lifted a hand in greeting. Bud grinned and nodded, but Nora only nodded, her face showing indifference. That graveled him for a moment, but then he remembered that Barney Ryan had mentioned some lies Jack Rawls had told. It was hard to tell what Nora Nelson believed about him.

When he topped the ridge, he saw the Bascom wagon stopped about fifty feet down the slope. Both Bascoms were on the ground staring at the heavy wagon. The lathered horses stood spraddle-legged, their heads down.

Bascom said, “We made a bad mistake, Mr. Jones. We’ll never get to Deadwood with this load.”

“You’ll do well to get to Pole Creek,” Dakota said. “If your horses have enough left in ’em to get over this hump, it’s downhill all the way to the creek. Tomorrow morning, Hargadine will see you get mules.”

“That is a pleasant thought,” Mrs. Bascom said. “My husband has a real affinity for mules, Mr. Jones.” She smiled energetically at her small spouse. “Isn’t that right, Hercules?”

“I ain’t above driving mules, Honey Doll,” Bascom said. “But I don’t think we’ll ever get to Pole Creek.”

“Of course we will, Hercules,” Mrs. Bascom said. “I think these old horses have rested long enough. Now you get back up into the seat and pick up the lines. I’ll go around on the other side and grab a wheel and give it a heave. We're over the worst of the grade. If it's downhill from the top to the creek, we'll make it before dark."

"Yes, dear," Bascom said, and stepped to the hub of a front wheel and on up into the seat.

"It's just a matter of getting it started, Mr. Jones," Mrs. Bascom said. "You want to give us a hand?"

"Sure," Dakota said.

He didn't think the horses had enough strength left to pull Bascom's hat off his head, but he gripped the spokes of the wheel nearest to him. Mrs. Bascom did the same on the opposite side.

Bascom spoke to the horses. They lunged into their collars, and Dakota strained. To his surprise, the big wagon creaked and groaned and began to move. Mrs. Bascom seemed to have a lot to do with it, somehow. The wheel made one complete turn, Dakota stepped back, and the wagon kept on moving. A short time later, it reached the crest. Bascom let out a whoop and stopped.

"We done it, Honey Doll," Bascom crowed. "Yes, sir, we done it. We'll camp down yonder with everybody else."

"We sure will, Hercules." Mrs. Bascom winked at Dakota. "Thank you, Mr. Jones." She strode ponderously up the slope, climbed to the seat, and sat down beside her husband. Dakota stepped into the saddle and turned his sorrel toward Pole Creek.

Chapter 7

Barney Ryan had supper ready by the time Dakota unsaddled and staked his sorrel out on the grass. Jack Rawls and the guards were camped downstream from Ryan's wagon. Their loud talk and laughter attracted Dakota's attention as he ate, so he watched. Presently, he saw a bottle being passed around.

"I know what you're thinking," Ryan said. "If Hargadine doesn't put a stop to that, there'll be hell to pay long before we get to the Hills."

Dakota nodded. "It probably doesn't make any difference tonight. I don't figure we're far enough north to have any Indians prowling around. But if they keep it up, Hargadine had better put a stop to it."

"He's a queer one," Ryan said thoughtfully. "Some ways he's tougher than a boot heel, but some other ways he's not. Now, if it had been me, I'd have been a little curious about this man who rode in a while ago, as close to Cheyenne as we are."

"I didn't see anybody ride in," Dakota said.

"You hadn't got back yet," Ryan said. "I don't know who he is, but that bunch of guards seem to know him. He's the one with his back to us. The big bastard. Wide as a house across the shoulders.

The guards had him sit down and eat with them. I don't know why he's here or what harm he can do, but it seemed queer the way they cottoned to him."

Dakota was holding a tin cup full of coffee in front of him, squinting over the rim. The big stranger turned his head to say something to Rawls, and Dakota got a look at his face for the first time.

"By God," he said. "It's Hemp Childers."

He tossed the tin cup to one side and came to his feet. He strode toward the guards' campfire, and his feet made no sound. The red-bearded guard, Summers, saw him coming. Summers said something to Childers, but he spoke too late. Dakota grabbed Childers by a beefy shoulder and hauled him around.

"I'm going to beat you to death, you son of a bitch," he said, and hit the man on the jaw.

Childers went back and down, his arms flailing in the air. He fell into the fire and let out a squall of agony and rolled away. Summers said, "If you're looking for a quick way to die, Jones, you found it."

Other men came running, the Burke twins in the lead. Jubal yelled, "Stay out of it, Summers!"

And Tubal, a step behind his brother, called, "You, too, Rawls!"

Childers was on his feet.

"Jones," he said hoarsely. "Dakota Jones."

Then he lowered his head and drove at Dakota like an enraged bull. Dakota didn't back up or sidestep. When Childers was almost on him, he raised a knee. There was a soggy, sickening thud. Childers spilled sideways, and Dakota fell on him, straddling his barrel chest. He hit him in the face three times, hard and heavy, closing an eye and smashing his nose and cutting his lip. Childers kept squirming and turning and bucking, but now Dakota had him by the throat, choking him.

Hargadine caught Dakota's shoulder. "Let him up. You hear me? Let him up."

Dakota finally did hear him. Childers was only half conscious, his face purple. Dakota rose and kicked him in the ribs. He said thickly, "Get him on his horse and get him out of camp before I do kill him."

Childers remained on the ground, moaning, struggling for breath, pawing his battered face. Rawls glared at Dakota but made no move. Summers said hotly, "He wasn't doing nothing. What the hell right have you got to butt in like this?"

Dakota wheeled. He drew his knife.

"Show me a better right," he said.

Summers looked at Dakota's face, then at the razor-sharp blade, shiny bright in the late-afternoon sunlight.

"I'll get his horse," he mumbled.

No one spoke during the time it took Summers

to saddle Childers' horse and lead it to the man. Childers lurched to his feet and wiped a sleeve across his blood-smeared face. He gripped the horn and stared at Dakota. Then he said thickly through swollen lips, "Someday I'll see you again, Jones. It'll be different then."

"It will," Dakota said. "It sure as hell will. If I ever get you alone, I'll cut you open from your throat to your crotch."

Childers pulled himself into the saddle. He rode away, hunched over, swaying. Then Rawls said, "All right, Jones. Why?"

Dakota turned to him.

"Rawls, you're an idiot to let a man like that come into camp. We don't want anybody counting rifles or looking into wagons to see what they're carrying. And Childers—"

"He was just riding through," Rawls said. "Summers knows him. They'd ridden for the same outfit on the Powder."

"And maybe both of 'em sold whisky to the Utes," Dakota said. "If Childers ever shows up again in Crow country, they'll cut him up an inch at a time. He raped and murdered a sixteen-year-old Crow girl."

He heard Hargadine and some of the others murmur in shocked surprise, but the crime meant nothing to Rawls and his guards. Rawls said, "There ain't no Crow girls in this outfit."

"There are white women," Dakota shot back.

"Childers belongs to the Pumpkin Butte gang of outlaws. They've been robbing and killing on the Cheyenne–Black Hills road since the first miner started north. Now that Childers has had a chance to look us over, they'll hit us somewhere north of Fort Laramie."

"I didn't know who he was," Rawls said, "or I wouldn't have let him stop."

"I didn't, neither," Summers mumbled.

Dakota grunted and spat on the ground. But he had no proof, so he walked back toward Barney Ryan's wagon. The Burke twins and Hargadine caught up with him. Dakota said, "How well do you know Rawls, Hargadine?"

"I don't know him at all," Hargadine said. "I mean, I didn't know him until I hired him three months ago, but he's worked hard for me getting this outfit together and hunting up guards and everything."

"How'd you happen to get hold of him?"

"Duke Wynne recommended him," Hargadine said. "I've known Duke a long time. A good wagon boss is hard to find, so I took Duke's word for it."

"You're gonna have to fire him," Jubal said. "If you don't do it now, you will by the time we get to Fort Laramie."

"You'll fire him or me," Dakota said grimly, "unless I kill him first."

"By God!" Hargadine roared. "Don't you give

me credit for enough sense to make my own decisions?"

"Not when it comes to a man Duke Wynne recommended," Jubal said. "Rawls is a bad one, but you've never been able to see it. If it ain't come to a head by the time we get to Fort Laramie, I'm quitting. I don't trust Jack Rawls no more than I'd trust a sidewinder in my blankets."

"If Jubal quits, I quit," Tubal said.

It was blunt talk, the kind Hargadine didn't like and wasn't used to hearing, Dakota thought. Well, he was tired of talking himself, for that matter. He walked on toward Ryan's wagon.

"Wait a minute," Hargadine said. "I haven't made up my mind about Rawls. Or about you, either. The other night in the saloon, you were a wild man. Today, you were sane enough until you recognized this fellow Childers. Then you went crazy again. Is it going to be like that all the way to Deadwood?"

"You ain't making sense, Sam," Jubal said. "You wanted Dakota bad enough the other night, and he was crazy enough to take on four men."

"He's a one-binge-a-year man," Tubal added. "If I'd knowed what he knowed about Childers, I'd have gone crazy, too, when I seen him."

Hargadine wasn't listening. He was staring at Dakota, waiting for his answer. Dakota said, "I guess you'll have to wait and find out," and left him standing there.

Chapter 8

Before Dakota went to bed, he walked upstream to the Bascom camp. The sun had been down for several minutes, and now the uncertain dusk light was rapidly turning to darkness. Mrs. Bascom was cleaning up after supper, and Bascom was returning from where he had staked out the horses.

"I saw what you did to that stranger," Bascom said. "You really threw the fear of God into Rawls and Summers and their crew. I didn't think it was possible."

"There's a lot of bluff in men like that," Dakota said mildly.

"To you there is," Bascom said in a low voice. "Not to me. They live on the level of animals. I've been the butt of their jokes and brutality too long."

Dakota studied the little man in the thinning light. Maybe there was more to Bruce Bascom than he had thought. He said, "I've seen a lot of men who made animals look good. Most of 'em white, too."

"Oh yes," Bascom agreed. "You remember I told you that I had traded some with the Utes in Colorado. That's when I first saw Summers and Laird. I know several of the Ute chiefs pretty well, Ouray and Shavano the best. They're fine men. As a matter of fact, I like Utes generally."

"I've never been around the Utes much," Dakota said, "but I know the Sioux and Cheyennes and Crows pretty well. Indians are like anybody else. Some are good, and some are bad."

"That's right," Bascom said. "They've had trouble with the whites, but the whites are greedy and strong, and most of the trouble is their fault."

Dakota nodded, thinking about the Sioux. Crook had been whipped, but the war would go on until the Sioux power was crushed, and in the end, Uncle Sam would find a way to give the miners a legal right to be in the Black Hills. That was the way it always had been and always would be. It made Dakota wonder whether the Sioux should send missionaries to the whites instead of the other way around.

"Well, I came over to ask about your horses," he said.

"They're about finished," Bascom said, "as far as pulling our wagon goes. Of course, you know Hargadine has promised us a team of mules in the morning. I've never handled mules, but I'll try. If I can't, Honey Doll can."

Dakota grinned. "I'll bet she can at that."

"We've built our dreams on the contents of that wagon," Bascom said gravely. "We both had a little money when we got married, and we invested all of it in merchandise. We plan to start a little store in the Black Hills. I don't know where, but we'll find us a gulch that's got some miners working it. Just so it's somewhere out of Deadwood. We don't carry luxuries. Just staples miners have to have—lard, sugar, flour, bacon, rice, and such."

Mrs. Bascom had come to the front of the wagon. She patted her husband on the back. "Hercules is a fine businessman, Mr. Jones. I'm sure he'll find a good spot for our store."

"Thank you, Honey Doll," Bascom said modestly. "I do pride myself on being a good businessman. If we hadn't had that awful panic three years ago, I'd be well off, and we wouldn't have to go to the Black Hills."

Dakota didn't think a good businessman would have put all of his money into merchandise and tried to haul it to the Black Hills with the team Bascom owned, but he didn't make the point.

"I wanted to ask you what we ought to do about the mules, Mr. Jones," Mrs. Bascom said, "I wondered if I should remind Sam Hargadine of his promise."

"I'll see you get them," Dakota said.

"Thank you, Mr. Jones," Mrs. Bascom said hoarsely. "You're a good man. I guess you're about the best man I ever knew next to Hercules."

She choked up and turned and walked away. Bascom said, "She gets kind of emotional sometimes. She's had a hard life, what with all kinds of mean things being said to her and done to her 'cause she's big. But there's nothing she can't do. The way she loaded this wagon was a caution. She toted sugar sacks out of the warehouse in Cheyenne and stacked 'em in the wagon like they was boxes of matches. I couldn't even lift one of 'em."

"Just to satisfy my curiosity," Dakota said, "why does she call you Hercules? You said your name was Bruce."

Bascom laughed softly. "Well, it's like this, Mr. Jones. I can't do much in a world of tough men, and Honey Doll, well, being so big and so damn strong, it's hard for her to be an ordinary woman—"

He paused, embarrassed, and Dakota said, "Go on."

"I found out a long time ago that most women won't look at me twice, and, of course, most men are scared of Honey Doll on account of she could slap one silly with the first whack, so I call her Honey Doll to make her feel proud of being my wife, and she calls me Hercules to make me think—"

"You two make a good team," Dakota said. "Well, I'll mosey back to Barney's wagon and see if I can get in a little sleep before Rawls yells that it's time to roll."

Approaching the Nelson wagon, Dakota saw

that both Nora and her brother were sitting by the fire. The girl spoke first.

"Rawls was right about one thing," she said. "We saw what you probably call a fight, Mr. Jones. You look like any other white man, but you really are the savage Rawls said you were."

Dakota considered telling her about the Crow girl Hemp Childers had raped and murdered, but maybe she wouldn't care one way or the other.

"Sure, I'm a savage," he said. "Did Rawls tell you I'm a cannibal, too?"

He went on to the Ryan wagon, thinking she would probably believe it. He was surprised to find Sam Hargadine sitting beside Ryan, a long cigar tucked into one side of his mouth. Hargadine motioned for him to sit down.

"Jones, Abby's been on my neck to tell you something that rightly ain't no business of yours, but I'm going to tell you to shut her up. I don't want to lose the Burke boys, either, and for some God-damned reason which doesn't make much sense, they cotton to you. They claim Rawls is out to double-cross me, though how they know that is something I haven't figured out. If it comes to having to choose between you, I'll take you."

"Don't go against your better judgment," Dakota said sourly.

"I won't," Hargadine said, "but it gravels the hell out of me the way the twins and Abby have ganged up on me. They seem to think they're better judges of human nature than I am. I've been a professional gambler for twenty years. If I hadn't learned to know people, I'd have been out of business a long time ago."

"One thing, Hargadine," Dakota said. "Why were you so anxious to hire me after you saw me have that fight in your saloon? You went to a lot of trouble and made me a big offer if you weren't dead sure I was a man you could trust."

"I knew you were a fighting man and that you knew Indians," Hargadine answered. "I figured I could leave everything else in Rawls's hands. But now it doesn't look as if I can. Your finding this man, Childers, in camp changes things."

He took the cigar out of his mouth and fingered the ash off the end. "You see, too much depends on this trip. I wasn't satisfied to stay in Cheyenne and play small. I had to have it big, so I mortgaged everything I own to put this outfit together. I want to get to Deadwood ahead of another saloon man named Jake Elling." He put the cigar into his mouth and pulled on it hard. "Elling and I have been out to beat each other for years. At one time, we had saloons across the street from each other in St. Louis. Someday I'll kill the bastard, but right now all I'm interested in is getting to Deadwood ahead of him. There is no first-class saloon in Deadwood, so whichever one of us gets there first will have a bulge on the other.

"I sent Duke Wynne to Sidney to find out what Elling is doing. If he hasn't started, we should beat him without trouble. I haven't heard from Duke yet, but I'm sure there will be a wire waiting for me at Fort Laramie. I guess what really screwed my nerves into a knot was the thought that Elling might have put this Hemp Childers up to visiting us and then dragging that pack of outlaws down on our heads. If Summers and maybe some of the other guards are in it with Childers, why, we're in trouble."

"You are in trouble, Hargadine," Dakota said. "We'll have to fight our way into Deadwood. You can count on it."

"You're a cheerful bastard!" Hargadine got up, his jaws gripping the cigar. "Oh, one more thing. The sack I showed you that has your pay in it is in one of Abby's valises. Ask her for it if I don't make it to Deadwood."

"I will," Dakota said. "And don't forget your promise to loan a team of mules to the Bascoms."

"I'll remember," Hargadine said, and strode away into the darkness.

Dakota looked across the dying fire at Barney Ryan. He said, "I'm hoping for a quiet day tomorrow."

"You won't have one," Ryan said. "I don't think we'll have a quiet day until we get to Deadwood.

Dakota, there's one thing Hargadine didn't tell you. This outfit was a week late getting out of Cheyenne."

"Why?" Dakota asked, but Ryan didn't know.

Chapter 9

Dakota woke suddenly, prickles of warning running along his spine. Someone was here. Close. His right hand eased his knife from the scabbard.

Slowly, he turned his head, opening his eyes as he slid the knife upward along his side. He glimpsed a shadowy figure bending over him. He rolled away and came to his feet.

"Dakota! It's me. Abby."

He caught the downsweep of the knife in time. "You fool woman," he breathed. "You know you almost got yourself killed?"

"So I see," she said shakily. "What did you expect me to do, beat a bass drum and wake everybody in camp?"

Dakota replaced his knife. He took a long breath and sat down. He said, "How long were you here beside me before I woke up?"

She sat down and moved very close to him. She whispered, "A few seconds. Keep your voice down. I don't want anyone to wake up and know I've been here. Sam in particular."

"You don't want to make Hargadine jealous. Is that it?"

She laughed silently. "Jealous? No, I'm afraid Sam would never be jealous. With Janie around, acting like a bitch in heat, all he needs is an excuse to throw me out. No, I've got something to tell you. I think you ought to know it, but for some reason Sam didn't tell you when he talked to you this evening."

She pressed so close to him that her mouth was within an inch of his ear. "I've been awake all night trying to make up my mind about telling you, and I finally decided I would, but don't tell Sam you know. He gets a little crazy when he thinks anybody is interfering in his business."

"All right, I won't tell him. Go ahead."

"He's a fool to trust Rawls," Abby said bitterly. "The twins and me both think Rawls aims to sell us out somewhere between Fort Laramie and Deadwood, but we can't prove it, so we don't say much to Sam about it. I think Sam realizes it now, but he's too stubborn to admit it and fire Rawls."

"This what you wanted to tell me?"

"No, I'm building up to it," she said. "You just let me tell it on my own windy way because there are some causes to Sam's stubbornness. The main one is that he trusts Duke Wynne. Sam is the kind who trusts a man all the way, and Duke has worked for him for years. Well, Duke recommended Rawls; therefore, Sam can't bring himself to get rid of Rawls no matter what he thinks."

"How come you and the twins are down on Rawls?"

"Because we don't trust Duke Wynne," she answered. "We know he's been cheating Sam, but we can't prove that either. When anybody goes to Sam with a story about Wynne, he'd better be sure he can prove it. The twins and me think Wynne has sold out to Jake Elling. That's why he wanted to hire Rawls. He did tell you about Elling, didn't he?"

"Yeah, he told me."

"Well, Jake Elling is the only man in the world Sam really hates. They've fought for years. I've got an idea this will end it. One of 'em will kill the other one in Deadwood. Or maybe they'll kill each other." Abby sighed heavily. "Another one he trusts is that Goddamned sneaky Janie. I know for a fact she'd sell him out for fifty cents. I think she has already."

"Abby, if you—"

"What I came to tell you is that Sam is taking fifty thousand dollars in gold to Deadwood. He figures he needs that much to run his games, which he aims to open as soon as he gets there. He says the big money is in gambling, and he'll double the fifty thousand in two or three months after he opens."

"Who knows about it besides you?"

"Nobody is supposed to," she said. "I hid it in a flour barrel in the supply wagon. We're taking more grub than we need because prices are higher'n a scared cat's back in Deadwood. Some of the supplies we marked to use on the road. The rest won't be opened until we get there. We figured that was the last place anybody would look. If outlaws hit us, they'll maybe try to take some grub, but it ain't likely they'll haul off anything as bulky as a barrel of flour."

"But you figure somebody knows, huh?"

"Somebody knows, all right," she said angrily. "That's why I'd like to cut that damned Janie's throat. She let something slip tonight to Jubal, and he told me. Like I told you a while ago, Sam's downright foolish with people he thinks he can trust. He don't know that Rawls spent a good part of last night with Janie, more'n was necessary for a professional visit, so it seems to me there's a good chance Janie told Rawls, and maybe Rawls told this fellow that you whipped tonight."

"And if Hargadine loses that fifty thousand dollars before he gets to Deadwood," Dakota said thoughtfully, "Elling has knocked him out before the fight starts."

"That's right," Abby said. "That's exactly right."

"Why tell me?"

She sighed. "I thought it might make some difference in the way you handled whatever we run into."

"You've got no way of knowing you can trust me," he said.

"I don't have no way of knowing," she admitted, "but I've got more'n my share of woman's intuition. I'd have come up missing more'n once if I hadn't. It's a hell of a tough world I've lived in the last twenty years, and I've learned there's times when you've got to trust somebody. You're the best bet I've got."

She paused, her face still close to his. Then she said, "I'll tell you something else. I'm holding the dinero Sam promised you, and by God, if you ever expect to see it you'd better pull us into Deadwood alive and kicking."

He grinned. She was a tough one. Sam Hargadine was lucky to have her on his side, whether he knew it or not.

"I'll remember that," he said. "Now you hike back to your tent before the camp wakes up."

She hesitated as if trying to make out his face in the starshine, but the light was too thin to see his expression. Without a word, she pulled away from him and disappeared into the darkness.

There was no more sleep for Dakota that night. He was still thinking about the fifty thousand dollars when the first dawn light began working into the eastern sky, and Rawls's great shout, "Roll out! Roll out!" woke the camp.

Chapter 10

Dakota had just finished saddling his sorrel when the big, red-bearded guard, Summers, drove a pair of mules to the Bascom wagon. He handed the lines to Bascom and wheeled away while Bascom was still thanking him. He stalked off, plainly indignant because he had been asked to do anything as menial as delivering the mules to Bruce Bascom.

Mrs. Bascom was packing up after breakfast, and she kept on until she finished the job. Dakota, watching Bascom try to hook up the mules, felt both amusement and sympathy. The little man honey-talked the mules; he begged them, he cursed them with considerable feeling, he slapped them with the lines, and finally, in desperation, he kicked one mule on a hind leg.

This was a mistake. The mule kicked back, and his hoof grazed Bascom's head. Bascom ducked and retreated, and then stood staring at the mules, completely defeated and close to crying. For the mules, it had not even been a good contest. They stood with their ears drooping, their gaze fixed on some distant point as if thoroughly bored.

Dakota considered taking over. He could get those jarheads into position and hooked up in thirty seconds. But he decided against butting in.

He couldn't be with the Bascoms all the time; it was something they had to handle.

Mrs. Bascom finished stowing away the grub and the pans and dishes. She kicked out the cook fire and walked along the side of the wagon, her big arms swinging at her sides. She said, "Are those pesky critters giving you trouble, Hercules?"

"They certainly are, Honey Doll. They won't let me hook them up. They just stand there."

"Now, Hercules," she said, "you never can afford to show any consideration for mules, not even as much as you'd give a rattlesnake. They'll take advantage of you every time. So let me take the lines, dear."

Bascom handed the lines to his wife and stepped back.

"If they were horses," he said, "I'd know how—"

"But they ain't, Hercules, so you can't treat 'em like horses."

Both mules had turned their heads to look at her. Their long ears tipped forward. They had recognized a worthy opponent.

"Now then, you long-eared sons of bitches," Mrs. Bascom said, "I ain't putting up with no more foolishness out of you. Just get it through your thick skulls that you're gonna do what I tell you." She then proceeded to curse them for two minutes in a vocabulary which would have done a professional mule skinner proud, and ended up with, "In case I ain't made myself plain, you God-damned, lop-eared offsprings of an unnatural union, I will now see that you understand."

The mules watched her intently.

She stepped forward and walloped the nearest mule on the rump with her open right hand. The animal jumped forward about two feet.

"Now you get over there where you're supposed to be before I get mad!" she bellowed. "If you kick me, I'll kick you right back, and you sure as hell will get the worst of it."

They believed her. In a matter of seconds, she had them backed up to the wagon; she hooked up and stepped away, nodding at Bascom. "Get up there on the seat, Hercules," she said. "From now on, they'll be the best-behaved mules between here and Deadwood. I'll tie the horses to the back of the wagon."

Dakota turned away, winking at Barney Ryan, who had already hooked up and was in the wagon seat, ready to roll. Ryan winked back. Neither said a word nor allowed himself the semblance of a grin. Dakota rode to the head of the column that was forming behind Hargadine. Jack Rawls said, "We'll make camp tonight on the Little Bear. It's a pretty short haul, but it's better'n making a dry camp, and it'll make an easier day to the Chugwater tomorrow than if we camp on Horse Creek."

Hargadine nodded. “Good,” he said.

Rawls scowled and stared across the prairie as if he wasn’t even aware of Dakota’s presence. Dakota cleared his throat.

“I don’t expect to run into any Indians for a few days,” he said, “but we’d better get some habits set right now. Don’t let anyone leave the train and go sashaying off across the grass. That’s the way people get killed.”

“I’ll take care of it,” Hargadine said.

Dakota put his sorrel into a trot, then pulled off the road and waited until the column was formed and Rawls waved the wagons into motion. The order was the same as the day before. Hargadine was in front on his black, the surrey behind him, the wagon with the tent and the women’s supplies next, and the other wagons strung out behind. Again Rawls and the guards rode as flankers.

Touching up his sorrel, Dakota rode north. He had once heard a stage passenger say that the hills here reminded him of huge pillows laid side by side close together, and it struck him that the description was a good one.

The breeze blowing eastward from the Laramie range was cool at this hour. A few white clouds were in the sky, and now and then one of them covered the sun for a short time, throwing a patch of shadow against the grass so that it gave the prairie a sort of dapple effect.

As on the previous morning, Dakota swung

back and forth across the road, but he found no evidence of horsemen. At noon he rode into Fagan's Ranche, a stage stop on Horse Creek. Mike Fagan had just finished a nine-room house. He furnished meals to travelers and had stable space for about seventy horses.

Dakota ate dinner at Fagan's, and when he finished he told Mike Fagan that he was scouting for a wagon train bound for the Black Hills. Fagan stared at him in surprise. "What in hell does a wagon train need a scout for? There ain't no Injuns in a hundred miles of here. Didn't you hear about General Crook's expedition? He'll run the Sioux clean up into Canada."

"Maybe you didn't hear the latest news," Dakota said. "Crook ran into the Sioux on the Rosebud and took a whipping."

"I'll be damned," Fagan said. "I thought this man, Crook, was a fighter. After the way he handled the Apaches—"

"Maybe he ran into more Sioux than he figured on," Dakota said.

"I'll bet he did," Fagan agreed. He scratched an ear, then added uneasily, "Here I was, figuring we'd seen the last of 'em around here."

"That's what I wanted to know," Dakota said. "You haven't seen or heard of any raiding parties lately on this side of the Platte?"

Fagan shook his head. "Not for weeks. That's why I figured they'd all pulled out. The Rosebud is a long ways from here. I still don't figure we'll have any trouble this far south." He grunted and changed the subject. "Your outfit gonna stay the night here?"

"No, we'll go on to the Little Bear," Dakota said. "It still makes a long day to the Chug, but it'd be a longer one if we stayed here."

"Yeah, reckon it would," Fagan said. "Well, we'll be glad to have you."

"I guess you've got plenty of business," Dakota said. "From what I hear, everybody's lighting out for the Black Hills."

"There's a passel of 'em going by here," Fagan said, "and it was the same thing all winter. You know, we had a March snow storm that sure stopped 'em. For two days we had folks sleeping all over the place. On the floor and out in the stable and everywhere else. You wonder how many of 'em are gonna hit it rich when they get there."

"You do for a fact," Dakota agreed. "Well, I'd better be moseying along."

He thought about what Fagan had said as he rode north. Thousands of men and some women were hellbent for the Black Hills, and if this gold rush went like others had, only a small percentage would find what they had come after.

He wondered about two men who owned wagons in Hargadine's train, Ira Starbuck and Len Akers. They had told him nothing about their business, but Barney Ryan said both men had been in the Hills and had made big strikes before the Army drove them out. Now they were on their way back with their families. The thought struck him that they as well as Hargadine might be of interest to Jack Rawls.

Dakota had not ridden more than half a mile when he saw someone riding along the crest of a ridge to his right. He thought he caught something familiar about the rider, but it didn't figure that anyone from the train would be riding out here alone. Hargadine would not allow it.

Still, the feeling that he knew the rider kept plaguing him, so he turned the sorrel and rode toward the ridge. A few minutes later he realized it was a woman. She must have seen him, but she did not change pace or direction. From the angle she was taking now, she would miss the camp site on the Little Bear by three or four miles.

He put his horse into a gallop. The woman continued just as she was, pointing more to the west than north. When he had cut by half the distance between them, he recognized Nora Nelson. Damn the girl. He'd given her credit for more sense.

When he pulled in beside her, she smiled at him.

"Good afternoon, Mr. Jones. How near are we to the campsite?"

He opened his mouth to tell her his frank opinion of her brains, but her smile stopped him.

He closed his mouth, swallowed, and said, "Not far. Just yonder a piece." He jerked his thumb to the east, swallowed again, and then his temper got the best of him. He shouted, "Do you know how big an idiot you are?"

She stopped smiling.

"No, I can't say that I do, Mr. Jones. Are you anxious to tell me?"

"I sure am," he said, making no effort to lower his voice. "I told Hargadine this morning when I left not to let anyone go sashaying off by himself. How'd you get him to let you do it?"

"Oh, I didn't ask him," she said. "I was bored sitting on the seat and eating the dust of all those wagons in front of us, so the first time we stopped, I saddled my horse. I rode beside the wagon a while, but when we got to some willows, I pulled out of the train and hid there until Hargadine was out of sight. Then I made a big half-circle till I got ahead of him. I guess he still thinks I'm with Bud."

"The next time you try a trick like that, you'll be heading back to Cheyenne," Dakota said. "Do you know it's stunts like this that gives the Indians cheap scalps?"

"Indians?" She laughed. "Down here just out of Cheyenne? Don't treat me like a child, Mr. Jones."

"You'll be treated like a child as long as you act like one. The way you're traveling, you'd have crossed the Little Bear three, four miles above where we'll be camped and you'd have got yourself good and lost by night. What do you think would have happened then?"

"Why," she said lightly, "I guess I just never thought about that."

"I ought to pull you off that horse and paddle your little behind," he said. "Don't you know that, if I hadn't found you, we'd have spent the night looking for you? Tomorrow, too, probably."

She sat very straight in the saddle.

"Mr. Jones, if you lay as much as a finger on me, I'll scratch your eyes out."

For an awful moment, Dakota was tempted to take her up on it. But the moment passed. He jerked his head eastward.

"Come on," he said. "We'll find the campsite and wait for the wagons."

Chapter 11

Nora Nelson waited with Dakota as the wagon train rolled down the slope toward the Little Bear. Hargadine touched up his black and came on ahead. He reined up in front of Nora.

"Just how did you get here, Miss Nelson?"

"I was riding," she said coldly, "and your scout," she jerked a thumb in Dakota's direction, "saw me and brought me here."

"I see." Hargadine's tone was colder than hers. "How about it, Jones?"

"She was riding, all right," Dakota said. "The way she was headed, come night, we'd all be out looking for her—if there was anything left of her to find."

"Why are you still trying to scare me?" Nora demanded. "I told you I knew there weren't any Indians this far south."

"Indians ain't all," Dakota said. "There's plenty of white renegades riding through the country. They don't always stay on the road, and some of them would enjoy meeting up with a lone white woman."

This was something she had not thought of, Dakota saw, and it jarred her. She said nothing, but Hargadine had been fighting his temper and losing the battle.

"You knew the rules," he said harshly. "You knew I wouldn't have given you permission to ride off by yourself. You could have made us lose a whole day if Jones hadn't spotted you, and I can't afford to lose a day."

"I'd have found the camp," she said half-heartedly. Then she added with more spirit, "I was tired of eating dust from all the wagons in front of me. I notice you keep *your* women up front so they don't have to eat dust."

"It's my wagon train," he snapped, "and the women are valuable to me. You're not. In the morning, you and your brother will turn back to Cheyenne."

Hargadine wheeled his horse and rode to meet Jack Rawls, who had moved out ahead of the wagons. Dakota said, "I'm sorry. I didn't expect him to order you back. I thought he'd give you another chance."

"You're sorry?" she said. "Well, I'll tell you something, Mr. Jones. I'm not going back to Cheyenne. I am going on to Deadwood even if Bud and I have to travel alone. You can tell that to your precious Hargadine."

Head high, she rode toward her wagon and reined in beside it, saying something to her brother. Dakota chewed on his lower lip a moment, and then, as Rawls motioned the wagons into position along the creek, Dakota rode to the Nelson wagon and dismounted.

“I’ll talk to Hargadine,” he said. “Maybe he’ll change his mind after he cools off—if you’ll agree to abide by the rules.”

“Sure, I’ll abide by the rules,” she said. “But it isn’t like you to take my part. I thought you were always on the side of your boss. That’s where your bread is buttered, isn’t it?”

“Aw, now,” Dakota said, “even a savage knows that some females are special cases.”

He led his horse to Ryan’s wagon. He said, “Barney, I figure Nora Nelson would be pretty good at handling them mules the Bascoms are driving.”

Ryan cuffed back his hat and scratched his head.

“What I mean is, maybe we can work up a switch. Bascom would get along fine with the Nelson horses and—”

Ryan shook his head.

“No, Dakota, it wouldn’t work. It makes an equation like this. Two mules plus one stubborn female human equal zero. You see, the plus sign has to be changed to minus when you add ‘stubborn’ to mules. That’s why you come out with nothing.”

“Oh hell,” Dakota said, and led his horse to water.

After supper, he found Hargadine talking to the Burke twins in front of the tent. The gambler had just lit a long, thin cigar. He took it out of his mouth and thoughtfully rolled it between his fingers.

"I was just talking about the Nelson girl," he said. "We are agreed that we can't keep her with the train. If we let one person flout our rules, all of them will."

"Now hold on, Sam," Jubal said. "You're putting words into my mouth. All I want is for Nora Nelson to promise to behave the rest of the way. If she will, I say to let her and her brother stay with us."

Tubal nodded. "That's what I say. You wanted some women to make this look like a family train, so what's the sense of throwing one of 'em out? What's more, that boy, Bud, stacks up like a lot of man."

Jubal jerked a thumb at the guards and teamsters who were hunkered around a cook fire with tin plates in their hands. "He's more use to us than any of them hardcases. If we have any trouble, we'll get their knives in our backs."

Dakota said nothing. He had expected to argue Nora's case just about the way the Burkes had stated it, but the twins were in a better position to convince Hargadine than he was.

But Hargadine was not convinced yet. He put the cigar back into his mouth and chewed on it, his eyes narrowed as he stared thoughtfully at the Nelson wagon. Finally, Dakota spoke.

"I just thought of something, Hargadine. Let's

ask Rawls what he thinks about sending the girl back to Cheyenne."

"Rawls?" Hargadine wheeled to glare at Dakota. "By God, I have quit asking that bastard anything. I've just about decided you're right about him. I may let him go when we get to Fort Laramie. I hate to lose the guards, though, and I suppose they'd go with him."

"Maybe I'll find some men at Fort Laramie I can hire," Dakota said. "If I do, they'll be men you can trust."

"What would Rawls say if we asked him?" Jubal asked softly.

"You know damned well what he'd say," Hargadine said. "He'd tell us to send the girl back pronto."

"Well then?" Tubal prodded. "I don't figure we'll be taking his advice, so let's keep the girl."

"You're pretty damned cute," Hargadine said. "All right, Jones, you go tell her she can stay with the train, but if she jumps the traces one more time, back she goes."

"I'll tell her," Dakota said, and a few minutes later, he did.

She stared at him coolly.

"I guess," she said, "I'm supposed to fall all over you and thank you for saving our lives."

"Oh, come on, Sis," Bud said. "The man's giving us a hand. I ain't anxious to make this trip by our lonesome."

"Yes, I'm very grateful," Nora said sarcastically, "and you can tell Mr. Hargadine we will obey the rules. It does surprise me, though, that a man who fights as well as Mr. Jones and who has been a squaw man—"

"All right," Dakota said. "You've heard what Jack Rawls said about me, and for some reason, you insist on believing it. But I can tell you a few things about Indian women that white women could imitate. For one thing, they're proud of being women."

"Oh, I'm proud of being a woman," Nora Nelson said bitterly. "Very proud. I didn't think you knew I was a woman."

"I don't believe you're proud," Dakota said. "I think you're jealous of men because you want to be a man."

Nora glared at him for a few seconds; then her face turned red, and she went back to putting supper things away. She seemed to have much to do, and she did it with a great deal of rattling and banging.

For a time, Dakota didn't move. Bud grinned at him.

"She's got the worst manners in Wyoming," Bud whispered, "but I sure thank you for getting Hargadine to change his mind."

"You're welcome," Dakota said.

He walked back to the Ryan wagon. Barney Ryan surveyed him critically.

"Well," Ryan said, "I guess there is no such thing as a placid love affair."

"Huh?"

"You two are in love with each other, aren't you?"

Dakota squinted at him in the thinning light. "Have you gone plumb out of your head, Barney?"

"Oh, I'm sane enough. As a matter of fact, I am a careful observer of human nature."

"Me stuck on that mule-headed female?" Dakota said. "Man, she's the last—"

"Methinks you protest too much, my friend."

"Me—what kind of lingo is that?"

"Shakespeare."

Dakota snorted. "He never met Nora Nelson."

Chapter 12

"We'll camp tonight on the Chugwater," Dakota said, "just above the Kraft road ranch. It'll make the longest day's travel we've had, but we've been on the road a couple of days. That ought to be long enough to shake us down, so I think we can do it all right."

"How long?" Hargadine asked.

"About two miles longer'n the first day that brought us as far as Pole Creek."

"No steep grades?"

"It's up and down about like what you've been over," Dakota told him.

"Then I guess we can make it," Hargadine said.

"I'll be on the Chug when you get there," Dakota said and turned north.

All through the day, he saw much evidence of travel to the Black Hills. Some men rode horses, a few led pack animals, but most traveled in wagons. Only a few were members of organized trains, and no train was so well organized as Hargadine's.

This probably meant that none of the wagons carried anything of great value that needed many men to protect it, but it also pointed to Hargadine's outfit as one that would be worth looting.

Late in the afternoon, Dakota rode down the long grade that flattened out to form the floor of the Chugwater valley. Here, the country was better timbered than the prairie the wagon train had been crossing since leaving Cheyenne. Steep bluffs rose on both sides of the valley. Along the edges of the stream were groves of cottonwood, willow, and box elder. Some of the last were unusually large with huge, twisted limbs.

Thickets of red willows grew on both sides of the Chugwater. Dakota knew that the Indians scraped bark from these willows and dried it in the sun and then smoked it in their peace pipes.

The Sioux and Cheyenne valued this country. It had been part of their hunting ground for years.

The mournful cry of doves came to Dakota, and, as he trotted across the grass-covered bottom, he heard the sweet song of a meadowlark. There were other birds here, too, robins and snipe and some he did not recognize, along with the owls that rested on fence posts and the hawks and occasional eagles that sailed overhead with hardly any movement of their outstretched wings.

Dakota saw the Kraft road ranch ahead of him. Dan Kraft had been here as long as anyone, somehow keeping on friendly terms with the roving Indian bands that appeared from time to time. An old mountain man who had settled down to hard work, Kraft ran a big herd of shorthorns and had put in an extensive irrigation system.

This was the kind of place Dakota hoped to own someday, but he wasn't sure where he could find one. He should have started looking ten years ago, as Kraft had, but he'd let time slip by. Now he would have to go deeper into the Rockies or on through them to the other side. All he knew for sure was that time had just about run out for him and men like him . . .

He heard a burst of gunfire. As nearly as he could locate it, the shooting came from inside the house. He was still about fifty yards from the buildings when a boy, nine or ten years old, darted out of the brush along the creek and ran toward him, screaming, "Help! Help!"

He was Jimmy Kraft, the only child the Krafts had, and Dakota, who had stopped here on a number of occasions, knew the boy pretty well. This wasn't like him. He was a small imitation of his father, tough and self-sufficient, a real frontier kid. But not today.

Today, Jimmy Kraft was just a terrified little boy. Dakota reined up and swung down. Jimmy grabbed him around the legs and hung on as hard as he could. He was crying and trying to say something, but Dakota could not make out any of his words.

Dakota pried Jimmy loose from his legs and knelt in the road beside him. He said, "Easy does it, Jimmy. You want help. I'm here to give it, but I've got to know what kind of help you need."

Still, Jimmy babbled incoherently. Dakota shook him.

"Stop it, Jimmy. You remember me. I'm Dakota Jones. I've stayed overnight at your place. I'm a friend of your pa and ma."

Jimmy swiped a grimy hand across his eyes.

"Ma, she's back in the brush along the creek. She's gonna have a baby, but them men came—"

"Where's your pa?"

Jimmy swallowed and finally managed to say, "He'll be back later tonight. He went to Fort Laramie."

"All right, your ma's in the brush along the creek, and the men came. Where are they?"

"In the bar," Jimmy answered. "They're drinking up Pa's whisky and shooting up the place and raising hell. One of 'em came back to the kitchen where Ma was and said they wanted women. I got a gun, but one of 'em took it away from me and hit me. He went back into the bar, and Ma and me ran out through the back door."

Dakota stood up and looked back along the road. The wagon train was coming down the slope, a long way off. He didn't have time to go back and get help.

"Ma and pa wanted another boy besides me," Jimmy was saying, "but Ma, she never could get one started until last winter. Now she's scared she's gonna lose the baby. The man who came into the kitchen grabbed her and tore her dress. He scared her something awful."

Dakota said, "Jimmy, look up the road. You see the wagons coming?" The boy nodded, and Dakota hurried on. "You go as fast as you can till you meet them. Tell the man on the black horse who's riding in front just what you told me, and say that your mother needs some women to help her. I'll go take care of them men meanwhile, but she's going to need some women. You savvy?"

The boy nodded. "I'll tell 'em," he said, and ran.

Dakota mounted. He rode slowly along the creek, looking for Mrs. Kraft. Jimmy had probably been with her when he saw Dakota coming. As he rode, he heard more shots from the house and roars of drunken laughter. Then he heard another sound from the brush along the creek—the groans and moans of a woman in the agony of childbirth.

Dakota stepped out of the saddle. Letting the reins drag, he ran along the stream until he saw Mrs. Kraft lying on the bank. She was turning and twisting, her hands clutching her swollen abdomen. Her dress had been ripped from the collar to her waist. Tears ran down her cheeks as she tried to hold back the moans, but her agony was too great.

Dakota knelt beside her in the grass. "Mrs. Kraft, it's Dakota Jones. Can I do anything?"

She turned her head and bit her lower lip.

"Nobody can do anything for me," she whispered. "I'm going to have my baby, and it's too soon. Too—soon."

"I'll take you into the house and put you to bed," he said. "But first, who's raising the ruckus in there?"

"Outlaws. Part of the Pumpkin Butte gang. They've stopped here before." She shut her eyes and bit her lower lip again as another spasm of pain took her. "I tried to get out through the back door as soon as they came in, but they wouldn't let me go," she said when she could talk. "They wanted whisky, only we don't open the bar in the daytime. Besides, I never tend bar, and Dan won't be home for two or three hours yet, so I asked them to leave. They wouldn't do it. One of them was a big, red-bearded man. He grabbed me and tore my dress and said, after they drank a while, they'd want some women. I said there weren't any women and he said I'd do."

She shut her eyes and clenched her fists until another attack passed.

"Jimmy got hold of a gun, but he didn't have time to use it. The red-bearded man took it away from him and hit him on the side of the head and knocked him down. They started serving themselves, and this time they let Jimmy and me go out through the back door. But this was as far as I could go. The pains started—and I guess that was when Jimmy saw you."

"I sent Jimmy to the wagon train to get help," Dakota said. "Now we'll see about old red-beard and his pals."

"You can't handle them," she whispered. "There are four of them."

"That's about what I figured," Dakota said.

He got up and walked toward the house.

Chapter 13

Dakota made two guesses as he approached the front door. First, someone had been watching him from one of the windows. Second, this whole thing was a scheme to kill him.

All right, he was doing exactly what they hoped he would. No subterfuge, no back doors; he was walking right in through the front door. If they had decided to smoke him down the minute he stepped through the door, he was a dead man. But that didn't figure, considering the kind of men they were. To shoot him down at once would be too easy. There would be no fun in it. They would drag it out; they would play cat and mouse with him—and if he was guessing right on that, he had a chance.

Just before he reached the door, he drew his gun. He slipped in fast and put his back to the wall. So far, so good.

These men were guards from the wagon train, all right. Summers was the only one he knew by name, but he recognized the other three. Summers and two gunmen stood, their backs to the bar, facing Dakota. The fourth guard was on his left, two or three feet from the kitchen door and at least thirty feet from the trio at the bar. He had a gun in his hand, but he couldn't be covered.

All Dakota could do was sense his movements and check him as often as possible out of the corner of his eye.

Summers apparently thought three guns were enough to take Dakota. He didn't bother to pick up his own revolver, which lay on the bar beside him. He was waving a bottle in his right hand and leering drunkenly at Dakota.

"Well, boys, our pigeon walks right in just like we figured he would," Summers said jubilantly. "We've been looking for a chance to smoke this bastard down, and here he is."

"Drop your guns," Dakota said, "or I'll kill every son of a bitch in this room. I'll give you five seconds."

For a moment, there was no sound, no movement of any kind. Then Summers dropped his right hand with the bottle to his side. He peered bleary-eyed at Dakota.

"My God, boys, he thinks he's got a chance with three guns on him."

They had figured him right, but only to a point. They had not expected him to have his gun in his hand when he entered the room; they had intended to hooraw him and, after they'd had their fun, to kill him without giving him a chance. Now, even a little drunk as they were, they seemed to realize he had walked into the room knowing what he would face. The raw nerve of the act stunned them for a moment.

Dakota waited. The tension grew tighter and tighter, like a taut rope that has had too much strain placed upon it. Then, having waited more than the five seconds he had given them, Dakota smiled. The man standing next to Summers blinked. Dakota's first bullet caught him under the hinge of his jaw, angled upward, and tore the top off of his head.

The other two gunmen fired, filling the room with echoing roars and billowing powder smoke. Both missed.

Dakota's next shot nailed the second gunman at the bar. The slug smashed his nose and tore through the back of his neck. For an instant, his inert body remained upright by the bar, and then he slid to the floor like a piece of wet wash.

Dakota heard the second shot from the man by the kitchen door. He felt the lead tug at his hat as he wheeled away from the wall. Firing as he turned, he hit the man in the right knee and knocked him off his feet. The gunman hit the floor, rolled, and fired. The slug burned a red-hot crease along Dakota's ribs, but now he had the split-second advantage that he needed. The next shot drilled the outlaw just above his right eye.

Dakota said, "Drop it, Summers."

Shocked sober, the big redhead had dropped the bottle and grabbed his gun off the bar. He had it in his hand, but he didn't fire.

Powder smoke filled the room like nostril-stinging fog. Dakota's tall figure loomed up vaguely as if he were a ghost. Suddenly, all the fight went out of Summers. He dropped his gun and raised his hands.

"I'd like to kill you," Dakota said. "If there ever was a man who deserved it, you're him. But I'm going to take you to Hargadine. Maybe he can find a limb he can hang you from."

Dakota jammed his gun into the holster.

"First, though," he said, "I'm going to beat you half to death."

He hit Summers on the chin with a driving fist that snapped his head back, then slammed him in the guts with a vicious right that brought a sick grunt out of him. Dakota stepped back and kicked him in the crotch. Summers bent forward, paralyzed, gagging, his hands dropping to his sides.

Dakota stepped in and brought his right hand down in a chop. The edge of the hand made a meaty thud as it connected with the back of Summers's neck. Summers toppled forward. His face thumped the floor. His body settled more slowly and lay still.

Dakota kicked Summers's gun across the floor. It took him a few seconds to find some short lengths of rope behind the bar and tie Summers's hands and feet, and then he ran out of the house.

Mrs. Kraft was moaning, twisting and turning with the waves of pain that wracked her body.

She seemed only half conscious as Dakota picked her up and carried her into the house, but in a way, that was a blessing. The bar looked like a slaughterhouse, with three dead men lying in grotesque positions on the floor in pools of blood, and it wouldn't help any for her to see them. He strode through the kitchen to her bedroom and gently lowered her to the bed. She clung to him, crying.

Somehow, he freed himself from her clutching fingers and ran back into the kitchen, his heart pounding. He was scared now, more scared than he had ever been in his life. He had never delivered a baby. All he could think of was to build a fire, heat water, and hope that somebody from the wagon train got here in time to take over.

He found wood and kindling behind the stove, along with a can of coal oil. He filled the fire box with kindling, poured coal oil over it, and touched a match to it. He quickly replaced the stove lid and, picking up the tea kettle, pumped it full of water and set it on the front of the stove.

That was when the pound of hoofs and the rattle of wheels came to him, the most welcome sounds he had ever heard. He ran outside just as the surrey pulled up in front of the house. Mrs. Bascom was driving. Abby sat beside her, white-faced and trembling from what had probably been the wildest ride she'd ever had. Nora Nelson sat in the back seat.

Dakota ran to the team and took the lines from Mrs. Bascom.

"She's in the back bedroom," he said. "Hurry!"

Abby was out of her seat and running toward the front door before Dakota finished talking. Mrs. Bascom took a little longer to heave her big body to the ground. Dakota reached out and gripped Nora's arm.

"Don't go in there," he said. "It's not a pretty sight. Let the older women—"

"I'm not a child," Nora said. "Will you please quit treating me like one?"

She jerked free and ran after the other women. Dakota stood motionless, watching her until she disappeared into the house. She was still fighting to demonstrate her independence—but this time she was right.

Chapter 14

Dakota unhooked the team and led the horses to the corral. Then he stripped gear from his sorrel and turned him in. He heard Mrs. Kraft screaming as he dragged the bodies of the three dead men into the front yard and covered them with canvas he found in the barn.

When he returned to the house, he saw that Summers was conscious. He cut the ropes and prodded the outlaw in the back with his knife.

"On your feet and out through the door," he said. "You make one wrong move, and you'll get this knife all the way."

Summers struggled to his feet, looking over his shoulder at Dakota. "Go ahead and let me have the knife," he said. "It'll be better'n hanging."

Dakota obliged him enough to draw blood. Convinced, Summers stumbled out through the front door and across the yard. The wagon train had reached the creek, and Rawls was motioning the wagons into position when Dakota halted his prisoner in front of Hargadine's horse.

"Jones," Hargadine said, "what the hell are you doing with that man?"

Rawls came on the run.

"Put that knife up, Jones. Have you gone loco?"

"Surprised to see me alive, Rawls?" Dakota asked.

"Yes . . . No. Damn it, put that knife up!"

Dakota obeyed. Then, stepping back, he drew his gun.

"All right, Rawls," he said agreeably. "I just shot three of your men."

"You *what?*" Hargadine demanded incredulously.

"I killed three of Rawls's men."

"You—you're crazy," Hargadine exploded. "You're—"

"Don't tell me I'm fired," Dakota said. "I might take your word for it. If I pull out and you keep Rawls, you'll never even make it to the South Fork of the Cheyenne." He rammed the muzzle of his gun against Summers's back. "Tell 'em what you aimed to do and then tell 'em what happened."

"Don't tell anybody anything," Rawls warned. "Nobody's gonna believe anything you say when you've got a gun in your back."

The rest of the men in the train had gathered in a circle around Dakota, Summers, Hargadine, and Rawls. The remaining guard, Laird, joined Rawls. A moment later, the Burke twins appeared, standing a few feet behind Rawls and Laird. Summers hesitated, his face contorted by the agony of indecision. Sweat broke through, pouring down his face. His eyes darted from

Hargadine to Rawls and back to Hargadine.

Hargadine seemed at a complete loss. Jubal said, "Better get his story, Sam. Looks to me like this is what we've been expecting."

"That's right," Tubal added. "By the time Dakota gets done with Summers, it'll be time to hang him."

"No," Summers said hoarsely. "It wasn't my idea. It was Rawls's. He said we had to get rid of Jones, and this was the best time to do it. Me and the three men who went hunting this afternoon—"

"Shut up!" Rawls bellowed. "They don't know nothing, you fool. Now shut up!"

Jubal's gun cleared leather before Rawls finished. He dug the muzzle into the wagon master's back.

"Let him talk, Rawls. His story starts off real interesting."

Summers drew in a ragged breath. He didn't look at Rawls again. Most of the time, he stared at the ground as he talked. "We was supposed to go to the Kraft road ranch." He jerked a thumb at the house. "We was to get the drop on Dan Kraft and tie him up or something, and then scare Mrs. Kraft by telling her we was gonna rape her. We didn't know she was gonna have a baby."

He stopped, head bowed as he dug the toe of his boot into the dirt.

"Go on," Dakota said.

"Well, we guessed Jones would get here ahead of the train. That's the way he had been doing, so we got here in plenty of time. Kraft wasn't home. We done a little drinking, and Mrs. Kraft and the boy went out through the back door to the creek. When Jones rode up, the boy ran out and told him what had happened, I guess. We was watching and we seen Jones coming. We figured to have some fun before—before—"

Summers's voice trailed off. Dakota didn't bother to prompt him.

"They laid a trap," Dakota said, "and three of them died springing it. That's about all, Hargadine, except for one thing. Mrs. Kraft knows Summers and the three that were with him. She says they've stopped here before. She knew them as part of the Pumpkin Butte gang. I told you Hemp Childers belonged to that bunch. Looks to me like that's all you need to show where Rawls stands."

"He's a damned liar!" Rawls howled. "I never heard of this Pumpkin Butte gang he keeps talking about. It wasn't my idea for them fools to lay a trap either. If they done it, it was their own idea."

Hargadine scratched the back of his neck. Dakota knew he was having a hard time making this decision, and he was a little surprised to find that he didn't care much either way. From now on, Hargadine would listen to him or to

Rawls; it had to be one or the other. If he didn't fire Rawls, it would be time for Dakota to pull out.

Then Hargadine noticed Jimmy Kraft standing beside Barney Ryan. He motioned to the boy. When Jimmy reached his horse, he said, "You heard what this man said. Is that about the way it happened?"

Jimmy nodded. "There was a little more. They'd all been drinking enough to get real mean. They wouldn't leave when Ma asked 'em to, and then that one," he pointed at Summers, "came back into the kitchen and said they wanted women and Ma said there wasn't any women, so that made him mad and he said she'd do. He grabbed her and tore her dress—"

"Looks to me like a hanging is in order," Jubal said.

"Sure does," Tubal agreed. "I got a rope in the wagon—"

"No!" Hargadine said sharply. "This is not a court, and we are not a judge and jury." He nodded at Rawls. "You're fired. Take Summers and Laird and git. I don't want to see you around this wagon train again."

For a moment, Rawls stood his ground, thick legs spread, eyes on Dakota, trying to decide whether to make a fight of it now.

Tubal laughed unpleasantly. "Go ahead, Rawls. If Dakota can smoke down three men while they're holding guns on him, I want to see how you make out."

Without a word to Dakota, Rawls turned to Laird.

"Let's ride," he said.

Laird nodded, and both men wheeled and walked toward their horses. Summers said, "You gonna let me go?"

Dakota holstered his gun. "Get your horse and vamoose. I'm guessing Rawls will take care of you."

No one spoke until the three men had ridden away. Then Barney Ryan said, "I'd like to see what Rawls will do to Summers for giving the scheme away."

"He'll kill him," Tubal said. "Kill him and hang his hide up to dry."

"Barney, I don't want Jimmy going back to the house till his dad gets home," Dakota said. "Will you look after him?"

"Sure will," Ryan said. "Come along, Jimmy. Let's take care of my horses, and then we'll see what we've got for supper."

Hargadine sighed.

"Well, Jones, who's going to be my wagon master now?"

"You'll be your own," Dakota said, "but there's one thing you can count on. You'll see Jack Rawls again before you get to Deadwood."

Later, when Dakota was eating supper with

Ryan and Jimmy, Abby and Mrs. Bascom returned to the wagons.

"Nora's staying to look after Mrs. Kraft a little longer," Mrs. Bascom told Dakota. "She's really good help, Nora is. Mr. Kraft got home a little while ago, so I reckon she'll be along purty soon." She paused, glancing at Jimmy, then she said, "The baby died."

She went back to her wagon to start supper. For a long time, Jimmy sat staring at his half-filled plate. Then he said, "Ma and Pa sure did want that baby."

Dakota said very little as he walked Jimmy back to the Kraft place. Dan Kraft met them in front of the house. He patted Jimmy on the back and said, "I'm proud of you, boy. Mighty proud."

"You've got a boy to be proud of," Dakota said.

"You go in and see your ma," Kraft said. "She's still feeling poorly, but she'll want to see you." After Jimmy went inside, Kraft said, "I sure am grateful for what you done, Dakota. I don't know how you managed it, taking on four of 'em."

"Just lucky," Dakota said.

Kraft was ten years older than Dakota, a man whose early years had been spent among the tribes. Now he studied Dakota for a long moment before he said, "Excuse me for butting into your business, but you oughta get married and settle down. I was about your age when I married

Lucinda, and the only thing I'm sorry for is that I didn't get started sooner."

"I've been thinking about it," Dakota said, "but a man like me don't always run into a woman like your wife just when he decides it's time to settle down."

"I was thinking about this here Nora Nelson," Kraft said. "She sure has been good help for Lucinda. I thought you'd been overlooking her maybe."

"Yeah, I sure had," Dakota said, just a mite testily. But then, being dutiful, he added, "I'm going to get my saddle horse out of your corral, Dan. Tell Nora I'll walk to the wagons with her if she's ready to go."

When he returned to the house leading the sorrel, Nora was waiting for him.

"Thank you for walking with me," she said. "After what happened to Mrs. Kraft today, I realize the danger for a woman alone."

"I'm glad it didn't turn out worse for Mrs. Kraft," Dakota said. "It could have."

"I know," Nora said gravely. "She wanted that baby so much, so very much. Now she'll have to go to Cheyenne to see a doctor. She's in kind of bad shape, I think."

They didn't say anything for several minutes. Then, when they were within a few yards of her wagon, Nora said, "I know now that in a country like this, you have to meet brutality with force.

I didn't understand that before. I didn't know human beings could be as bad as those men were today."

She turned toward her wagon. She had come as near to apologizing as she was capable of doing.

Chapter 15

It was not Sam Hargadine's voice, but Jubal Burke's that called at dawn, "Roll out! Roll out!"

Dakota was not surprised. Sam Hargadine had somehow kept himself as immaculate on the road as he had in the Palace in Cheyenne, and now he would go right on in his usual style, the style of easy-riding comfort, with Abby as his valet and Jubal as his acting wagon master. If men were cats, Hargadine would be a pedigreed Persian.

When the wagons were ready to roll, Dakota rode to the head of the train.

He said, "We'll camp at Eagle's Nest tonight."

"How far?" Hargadine asked.

Dakota shrugged. "Twenty-five miles. Maybe less." He glanced at the clear sky. "You won't have any trouble making it as long as the weather stays this way. If we get a soaker of a rain, we'll be slowed up."

"I won't let it rain," Jubal said with a straight face. "I'm gonna keep it like this all the way to Deadwood."

"Good," Dakota said. "We could use some fresh meat, Hargadine. So far, I haven't brought any in, and maybe I won't. Not enough anyhow. You can buy as many antelopes as you want for one dollar a piece when you get to John Hunton's ranch. I've seen as many as a hundred of 'em hanging up there."

"Good idea," Hargadine said and added fretfully, "I wish we had some outriders."

"We'll pick up a couple when we get to Fort Laramie," Dakota said.

He glanced back along the line of wagons. Abby was driving the surrey and Tubal was in the wagon directly behind the surrey as he had been the three previous days. Dakota nodded at Jubal and touched up his horse. Jubal raised his right hand high, then whipped it forward, and the train got under way.

For several miles, the road followed the valley of the Chugwater to Chimney Rock. John Hunton's ranch, Bordeaux, was four miles farther north. Dakota stopped there for dinner and visited with Hunton, noting that a dozen or more antelope carcasses were hanging on the shady side of a shed.

Dakota told Hunton about the train he was guiding, and asked, "Any Indians around these days?"

Hunton shook his head. "Not that I've seen, but don't count on it being that way on the other side of the Platte. A lot of the Sioux will be heading back for the Red Cloud Agency, and you'll be damned lucky if you don't run into some of 'em."

Dakota nodded, then motioned toward the road

with a dust cloud hanging above it in the noon air.

"There is one hell of a lot of travel toward the Hills even with the Indian trouble that's going on. Do you hear anything about what they're finding up there?"

"Oh, there's gold in the Hills, all right," Hunton said. "But fellows like the one you're scouting for will wind up with all of it. Happens every time."

"It sure does," Dakota said, and wondered if Hargadine would live long enough to cash in on that sure bet.

Another four miles brought him to Chug Springs, and after that another seven miles to Eagle's Nest, a sandstone cliff that lifted fifty feet or more above the road. Dakota dismounted and staked out his sorrel and waited for the wagon train. He amused himself by studying the names and dates that had been cut into the face of the cliff, some going back to 1834. A good many of the names belonged to men he had known at one time or another.

The wagons rolled in late in the afternoon. "No trouble," Hargadine told Dakota almost as if he were surprised.

"You're not in trouble country yet," Dakota said. "You will be north of the Platte. I'll stay closer to the wagons then, and we'll corral every night. You'll get your share of trouble before you see Deadwood."

Hargadine drew a slender cigar from his pocket and bit off the end. He watched Jubal moving from wagon to wagon making an evening check, and then said, "Jubal will do fine."

"Sure he will," Dakota said. "Damn it, you sound like you're not real sure, yet you did right firing Rawls."

Hargadine surprised him by grinning. "I hate to admit I was wrong, that's all. Like I told you, I hired Rawls because Duke Wynne recommended him. Maybe Duke didn't know him very well."

"Maybe not," Dakota said and walked away.

The gambler irritated him. Loyalty to a friend was fine and dandy, but Hargadine carried it to the point of being ridiculous. Dakota was tempted to go back and tell him Wynne was where the trouble had been all the time, but Hargadine wouldn't believe him. Dakota wondered what it would take to convince him that Wynne was selling him out.

Tubal had started a fire for Abby, who was bending over it, frying pan in hand. Neither Janie nor Sweet Betsy was in sight. They were probably in the tent which Tubal had put up just beyond the wagon.

Dakota hunkered beside Abby. "Looks to me like you'd better make your two gals give you a hand. No work, no eat."

"Oh, they work." She brushed a lock of hair out of her eyes. "I'm a very peaceful woman, Dakota.

I try to get along without any fussing, and by God, you'd sure have to do a lot of fussing if you got any work out of either Janie or Sweet Betsy. With their hands, I mean."

Dakota laughed softly. "I'm glad you're a peaceful woman," Dakota said. "I had the idea before we left Cheyenne that you and Mrs. Bascom might tangle. But when it came to helping Mrs. Kraft, you two were right in there doing all you could like a couple of old pals."

"Yeah," Abby said. "That was a funny thing now, wasn't it? She figures she's a hell of a lot better than me because she and that runt husband of hers stood up before a preacher and had him say a few magic words over 'em. I love Sam, ornery as he is. I love him just as much as she loves her little man, but we didn't have a preacher mumble over us, so that takes away my respectability."

Dakota chuckled. "Don't tell me you're losing sleep over any lack of respectability."

"Hell, no. But it's something most women think is important." She paused, suddenly thoughtful. "You know, that Nora Nelson is a fine girl. She did more for Mrs. Kraft than me and old Elephant Bascom put together. You'd better not let her get away from you, Dakota Jones."

He stood up and glared at her.

"You, too?" he said bitterly, and got out of there.

He strode toward the Ryan wagon, hoping Barney had supper ready.

"Dakota."

He had not realized he was passing the Nelson wagon. He paused, facing Nora and hoping she didn't realize he was angry. She'd probably ask him why, and he wasn't going to give her the satisfaction of telling her.

"Well?" he said and scowled for good measure.

"Heavens!" she said. "I didn't aim to make you mad."

"You didn't." Suddenly, he laughed, deciding he might as well bring it out in the open. "It's just that people keep telling me I ought to marry you. I'll decide a thing like that myself."

If she was surprised, she didn't show it. She said, "It's ridiculous, isn't it? Why, we've only known each other four days, and they tell me the same thing." Abruptly, she giggled. "Who told you this time?"

"Abby."

"Well! I didn't know *she* was concerned about marriage."

"I think she'd believe in it if she could hog-tie Hargadine," Dakota said, and this brought on another giggle, followed by an awkward silence.

"I stopped you to ask the name of that mountain we see west of here," she said, recovering. "It stands up so much above the rest of the range that I thought it must have a name."

"It's Laramie Peak."

"Oh, I should have guessed that." She cocked her head, very cool and ladylike now. "About our previous conversation, Mr. Jones. You do kind of grow on a person, but I guess we would never agree on Indians. I still say they are savages."

"Of course, they're savages," he said. "But—" He paused, seeing that she was laughing again. She had baited a trap, and like a fool he had taken the bait. "You probably still class me with them, too."

He walked on to the Ryan wagon, but for some reason, he wasn't as mad as he usually was. He guessed she was a challenge to him, the same kind of challenge that gentling a horse to ride would be. He'd gentled plenty of horses, but a woman like Nora Nelson! He shook his head and thought about other things.

Chapter 16

Everyone had been looking forward to the overnight stay at Fort Laramie. It was beyond doubt the best-known stop on the Cheyenne–Black Hills road, and for years before this, it had been an equally well-known trading post on the Oregon Trail.

But there would be no time to rest or see anything. Jubal Burke announced that the train would not lay over a day as some had expected. If anyone needed supplies, he would have to get them that evening.

Before Dakota rode out that morning, he sensed a nervousness in Hargadine that had not been there before. As he trotted on ahead, he remembered that Hargadine was hoping a wire would be waiting for him at Fort Laramie from Duke Wynne telling him whether his rival, Jake Elling, had left Sidney. Dakota figured the wire would be a lie, but Hargadine would believe it.

For hours, Dakota rode through low hills covered by sagebrush. Before noon, he passed Six Mile Ranch, which was a relay station for the Cheyenne-Black Hills stages and had the reputation of being the bloodiest place on the road. Dakota knew of at least six men who had been shot to death here. He didn't know any reason for it unless it was the fact that a hog ranch was located here.

Dakota saw several of the women outside sunning themselves as he rode past. They waved and called to him, but he only waved back and kept on going. They were old and worn, a sorry lot who habitually wore soldiers' clothes which added nothing to their appeal, an appeal which became even less when they were compared to Abby, Janie, and Sweet Betsy.

Later in the morning, Dakota crossed the Laramie River to Three Mile Ranch on the north bank. Here was a small town with a number of buildings, including a store, a blacksmith shop, and a bunkhouse. Almost anything could be bought here that a pilgrim on his way to the Black Hills would need. Dakota knew both Adolph Cuny and Jules Coffey, who had started the place three years before. He tarried a few minutes after dinner to visit with them.

He didn't bother to ask about Indians this close to Fort Laramie, but he did ask about Jack Rawls.

"Yeah, we know him," Cuny said. "He stopped here with a couple of other men. One of 'em looked like he'd had hell beaten out of him."

Then Coffey said hesitantly, as if not sure he should say it, "They all got pretty drunk, Dakota. Rawls was mad. The drunker he got, the madder he got. He said you'd be along and we'd better get anything we could out of you because you weren't going to live very long."

"Is he fixing to attend to it personally?" Dakota asked.

"That's the way he was talking," Coffey said, "but he didn't say when or how. Was I you, I'd keep my eyes peeled."

"I'll do that," Dakota said.

As he rode on to the fort, he told himself there was nothing new in what he had learned from Jules Coffey. He had been dead sure right along that the Pumpkin Butte gang would hit the train somewhere north of the Platte. Now he had a feeling it wouldn't be very far past the river.

He reached the fort early in the afternoon, a collection of buildings sprawled on the prairie in a sort of bowl surrounded by low hills. Most of the buildings were constructed of adobe and stone, but others were frame, and a few were made of concrete.

He rode past the Rustic Hotel on his left, which was the headquarters of the stage company, and went on to the sutler's store and dismounted. He tied and, as he turned toward the door, he heard someone yell, "Jones! Dakota Jones! What the hell are you doing here?"

He wheeled toward the row of buildings that flanked the parade ground, most of them officers' quarters. One was Old Bedlam, a reddish-brown building with white trim, probably the most famous structure in the fort. A moment later, he recognized Captain E. B. Monroe, who was limping toward him. Monroe had been with Custer on his Black Hills expedition, and Dakota had become well acquainted with him.

Dakota hurried toward the captain and shook hands with him. "I guess I could ask the same question of you," he said. "I figured you'd be somewhere up on the Tongue or Rosebud or wherever Crook is."

Monroe scowled. "I wish to hell I was. The only way a man gets promoted is by fighting, not by nursing a damned gimpy leg in a fort. My horse piled me last April and busted up my left ankle, so when Crook came by here, I wasn't in any shape to go with him."

He shook his head. "A lot of my friends are up there. Royall. Henry. Vroom. Mills. A lot more. Henry got shot to pieces. The last I heard, they didn't expect him to live. Well, I don't know why we're standing here. Come on. We'll go to my quarters and have a drink. I have a bottle of good stuff I've been saving for special occasions."

Dakota walked beside Monroe to his quarters, which made up half of one building at the far end of the parade ground. Dakota told him why he was here, ending with, "I didn't think we'd run into any war parties this far south. Still, a man's a fool to try to guess what Indians will do."

"We send out patrols every day," Monroe said.

"We haven't run into any hostiles for weeks, but you're strictly right about not trying to outguess them."

He motioned to a chair. Going to a sideboard, he picked up two glasses and a bottle of whisky and brought them to the oak table in the middle of the room. He poured and handed a glass to Dakota.

"Custer tried guessing when he went into the Black Hills two years ago," Monroe went on. "He expected a big fight with the Sioux and was actually hoping for it. You know that better than I do. But the point is, the Indians didn't do what he thought they would. No doubt the same thing happened to Crook on Rosebud. Of course, he's a solid officer and not a glory hunter like Custer, but I think he ran into more Sioux than he figured on and took a whipping because of it."

"What's Custer up to now?"

Monroe shrugged. "Who knows? You can count on just one thing. He'll find a fight this time because he's in a hell of a fix politically, and he needs a big victory to come out on top. Now that Crook got trimmed, a win for Custer would make him look fine. Real fine."

"The whole thing stinks," Dakota said hotly. "The Black Hills belong to the Sioux, and there's nothing the government can do to change it."

"Nothing legally," Monroe agreed, "but on a practical basis, they'll change everything. You see, Terry is coming up the Yellowstone with a big column. I guess Custer is with him. Gibbon is coming in from the other side. So with Crook moving up from the south, they figured to catch the hostiles in a pincer movement—"

Dakota laughed and slapped his leg. "Only Crook took a licking. Well, by God, it serves 'em right. All we need now is for the Sioux to turn around and handle Custer the same way."

"They won't," Monroe said. "They're good fighters, sure. They've proved it often enough. But they're too individualistic. They can't or won't hang together long enough to plan and execute a campaign. Now they'll scatter, and some will head for Canada, and others will try to slip back to the Red Cloud Agency and act innocent. They're the ones you'll hit up there somewhere around Hat Creek."

"We're expecting it," Dakota agreed, "so we'll be ready for them. We've got enough rifles to fight off anything but a big bunch, and I don't think they'll travel in big bunches now." He rose. "Well, I've got to get over to the sutler's store or the hotel. I need to pick up a couple of outriders."

"You'll find them," Monroe said. "We've had several good men hanging around the fort hoping to catch on with the Army or an outfit like yours."

Dakota shook hands with Monroe and left his quarters. A brisk wind had sprung up, and as Dakota walked along the side of the parade ground, he heard the halyards make a noisy, slapping sound against the flagpole. When he reached the sutler's store, he saw the wagon train pulling into the grove of cottonwoods on the north side of Laramie River. Hargadine's black horse was tied at the hitch rail of the store. Dakota glanced along the bar until he spotted the gambler.

"You must have come on ahead of the wagons," he said.

Surprised, Hargadine wheeled around. Grabbing Dakota's shoulders, he shook him with the wildest kind of enthusiasm.

"We're all right, Jones! We're in good shape. I had a wire from Duke Wynne. It was waiting for me when I got here. Jake Elling is still in Sidney and doesn't plan to leave until next Monday. How far are we from Cheyenne?"

"About a hundred miles."

"Well then, we're that much ahead of him, and he'll never catch us." Hargadine dropped his hands to his sides. "I've been sweating over this more than I let on. If Elling had left Sidney when we did, or maybe even before, he'd have beaten us there." He wiped his flushed face with a linen handkerchief and turned to the door. "I'm going to tell Abby and the twins. They were about as anxious to hear from Duke as I was."

Dakota watched him saunter elegantly through the door, then turned back to the bar, thinking that

Jake Elling was probably halfway to Deadwood by this time, and Hargadine was already beaten. In any case, there was nothing he could do now to change things. The wagon train was moving about as fast as it could.

Dakota had not noticed any of the other men at the bar, but in a moment of silence, he heard one of them say, "Who's that handsome gent that's all dressed up in new buckskins? The one standing yonder at the end of the bar. The one that's smelling sweety nice."

"Handsome?" another man said. "Yore eyes are sure going bad, Squint. Worse'n I thought. That's the ugliest man I ever seen. I ain't even sure he is a man. I think they brought in a goriller from Africky and dressed him up in buckskin."

Dakota grinned at Squint Ballard and Dogface Malone, two mountain men he had known for years. They were bearded and dirty, apparently dressed in the same greasy buckskins they had been wearing the last time he'd seen them a year ago on the Pope Agie. He walked to them and cuffed them on the shoulders while Squint Ballard let out a great bellow and pounded him on the back and called for a new bottle of whisky.

"It ain't every day you run across a feller like Dakota Jones all decked out in new buckskins!" Ballard shouted exuberantly. "What the hell happened to your old outfit? The last time I seen you, it was just getting broke in good."

"You wouldn't believe it if I told you," Dakota said. "I should have known who was here. I caught that smell when I first came in."

"That's me," Malone said proudly. "Yes, sir, just like an old dog rolling in a rotten buffler carcass. It'd spruce you up some if you done likewise."

Dakota wiped his mouth with the back of his hand.

"You boys looking for a job?"

"That we are," Malone said. "For some fool reason, the damfool Army passed up the two best men around. Why, if we'd been with Crook—"

"I'm scouting for a wagon train bound for the Black Hills," Dakota said. "We need two outriders, men we can trust. You want the job?"

"There's one thing I don't savvy," Ballard said. "If they want men they can trust, how'd you ever get the job?"

"I sneaked in when they weren't looking," Dakota said. "How about it?"

"Sure, we'll take it," Malone said. "We ain't had nothing to eat for three days except rattlesnake meat."

"Now about this bottle?" Ballard held it up and stared at it speculatively. "You reckon we can get drunk on it?"

"No," Malone said happily, "but let's try."

Dakota sighed, wondering what Hargadine would say when he got into camp. Nora, too . . .

Hell, it didn't make one bit of difference what Nora thought.

Not one bit, he told himself as Ballard handed the bottle to him.

Chapter 17

When Dakota awoke the next morning, he wondered whether his head was all in one piece or not. It felt as if it had been split by an ax. He struggled to his feet and stumbled to the river. He knelt beside the stream and sloshed water over his face. When he returned to the wagon, Barney Ryan handed him a steaming cup of coffee.

Dakota gulped two cups, then got Ryan's face in focus.

"You're a magician to get coffee cooked this quick after Jubal hollered," he said. "Else you've been up all night boiling that stuff. It'd take the hair right off the back of a dog. Tastes like gunpowder diluted with a little water, by God."

"That's it," Ryan said, "and I've been up for two hours cooking the stuff. Now that we're getting to where we'll meet up with the Indians, I figured you'd better be in shape to earn your money."

Dakota grunted. "What happened?"

"Happened? Well, in a few simple words, Jubal had to haul you in from the fort last night. Hargadine would fire you if he had anybody to take your place. Man, I've never seen a drunker drunk than—"

"What did Nora say?" Dakota shook his head,

then moaned. "No, maybe you'd better not tell me."

"That's right. I don't think you want to hear it."

Dakota took a long breath and reached for the coffee pot. "Go ahead. I'll brace myself."

"Well, one of the kinder things she said was that you were disgusting."

"Was I? I mean, really dis—"

"You were," Ryan said. "And as for those two—two *savages,* as Nora puts it—that you brought with you!" Ryan shook his head. "Where did you find them?"

"Under a rock," Dakota said sourly. "What the hell, Barney? They're honest, and they won't cut your throat while you're asleep, which is more than you could say for Rawls and Laird and that bunch."

"That is barely possible," Ryan agreed. "But meanwhile, we have to look at them and smell them."

"How about that bacon?" Dakota said irritably. "I didn't know you were such a dude, Barney. You should have seen me before they cleaned me up. It's a kind of habit a man gets into when he's been in the mountains a long time. There isn't much incentive to live any other way."

"You've got an incentive now," Ryan said.

"What?"

"Nora."

Dakota sighed. Everybody in this wagon train

was going to have him married to Nora if they had to use shotguns to do it.

After choking down a little food, he saddled his sorrel and rode to the surrey. Jubal had just finished hooking the team to the surrey and was going after his saddle horse. Squint Ballard and Dogface Malone were saddled and ready to ride. Hargadine was holding the reins of his black horse as he stood talking to Abby, but he saw Dakota ride up and he raked the rascal with an accusing glare.

"I thought we had an understanding about your drinking, Jones. If I remember correctly, you said you wouldn't touch a drop all the way to Deadwood or something like that."

"That was Tubal talking," Dakota said easily. "I forgot to tell you that all bets are off when we're at a fort. You were safe here last night."

"It's still a long ways to Deadwood," Hargadine said. "I won't stand for drunkenness in a man who is responsible for our safety."

There was a moment of silence then. It grew tighter and tighter as Jubal rode to the surrey and Tubal walked up from the wagon behind the surrey. Ballard and Malone were grinning. The whole wagon train watched Dakota to see what he was going to do.

He leaned forward, one hand dropped over the saddle horn.

"Hargadine," he said, "any man who would

hire a wagon master like Rawls on Duke Wynne's say-so is a complete damn fool. All I did was lower my guard among friends in a safe place. Also, I'll get over being drunk in an hour or so—but you'll have a lifetime and still die a fool."

Hargadine's face turned white. He started to reach for his gun but changed his mind. He said hoarsely, "You're fired, Jones."

Dakota nodded. "Come on, boys."

He reined his horse around and rode off, Malone at his side. Ballard said, "Well, that was the shortest job I ever had," and followed them.

"Wait up," Jubal called. "I'm riding with you."

"Me, too," Tubal said.

"Oh, come on back, Dakota!" Abby shouted. The five horsemen drew farther away and her voice rose to a scream. "Sam! Sam, call these boys back before you lose your whole outfit!"

Dakota rode another ten yards before Hargadine called, "All right, Jones. It's your hand. I'm throwing mine in."

Dakota jerked his head at Malone and Ballard. "We are rehired, gentlemen," he said, and rode back to where Hargadine stood beside his black horse.

"Hargadine, we're camping tonight at Raw Hide Buttes. That's about twenty-four miles from here. It's just a hunch, but I look for Rawls to make his move between here and there. If he don't, he'll make it tonight after we're camped.

So we'll corral and put guards out. We'll do the same every night between here and Deadwood."

Hargadine cleared his throat. His face was still red, and he was having trouble breathing. Finally, he said, "All right."

"I won't be riding very far from the train today," Dakota said. "Malone and Ballard will ride on each side not more than a mile or two from the train. If you see me or one of the flankers coming on the run and waving his hat, you're to corral. You understand, Jubal? Don't wait to see what we've seen. Get the wagons circled pronto."

"Pronto it is," Jubal said.

Dakota nodded and touched up his horse.

Two miles from the fort the train crossed the new iron bridge over the North Platte, the hoofs of the horses and mules beating a hollow tattoo on the plank floor. The river was in flood stage, lapping at the willows growing high on the banks. Then they rolled out across the valley and well before noon started the climb that led to the top of the long ridge north of the Platte.

They passed Ten Mile Ranch, and four miles farther on moved by Government Farm where the Army had carried on experiments several years before to see if vegetables and grains could be raised for the soldiers. It had been given up as a failure.

Now the road ran through a series of hills carpeted by buffalo grass and a good deal of cactus and Spanish bayonet. There were numerous prairie-dog towns, the dogs standing up like tiny pegs pounded into the ground until they took warning and dived into their holes.

The Raw Hide Buttes lay west of the road. Here was a stage station on Raw Hide Creek near the base of the buttes, which had more timber than Dakota had seen for a long time. Dakota selected a camping place along the creek where there was still a fair amount of grass and signaled the train to form a circle, tongue to tailgate.

"We'll drive all the stock inside the circle as soon as they've grazed a while," Dakota told Jubal, and turned his sorrel toward Malone, who was coming in from the west.

"See anything, Dogface?"

Malone reined in close and lowered his voice. "I seen some riders while ago. Mebbe it didn't mean nothing, but they was sure keeping away from me. I'm guessing they're watching us from the timber on the buttes. I counted six of 'em."

Dakota nodded. "That'll be Rawls, though I figured he'd have more men. That's why he hasn't hit us in daylight, so we'll see them before sunup."

"What could six men do to a wagon train this size?" Malone asked.

"Quite a bit if they surprised us and it was dark," Dakota said. "Besides, we don't know that's all of the outfit."

“No, we don’t for a fact.” Malone scratched his neck, his eyes narrowing. “I don’t savvy, Dakota. What’re they after, our horses?”

Dakota hesitated.

“We’ll have to wait and find out,” he said.

Chapter 18

After supper, Dakota hunkered by the fire for a time, smoking and thinking. Finally, he knocked his pipe out and said, "Guess I'll go talk to Nora."

Ryan regarded him with great concern. "The moth," he said sadly, "is so drawn by the flame that he dives into it and is consumed."

"Very funny," Dakota said and walked away from him.

Nora was sitting by the fire, darning a pair of Bud's socks. She glanced up at Dakota and immediately returned her gaze to the darning egg.

Dakota sat down beside her. He said, "Good evening, Miss Nelson."

She continued to darn. Bud appeared from the other side of the wagon. He said, "Don't pay no attention to her, Dakota. She's got a mad on."

"Mad?" Dakota said. "What brought on a condition like that?"

"She didn't like seeing you drunk last night."

"Couldn't she shut her eyes and not see me?"

"I told her to do that," Bud said, "but she said that whenever you were around, she just couldn't keep her eyes off of you."

"I never said anything of the kind!" Nora

snapped. "I find it very easy not to look at him, especially when he's in the condition he was in last night."

"Don't you believe her, Dakota," Bud said. "She just don't want you to know how she feels. Why, every time you show up—"

"Bud," Nora said ominously, "it's time for you to report to Jubal Burke."

"Yeah, I guess it is," Bud said, grinning at Dakota. "Jubal put me on the first guard shift. He seems to expect trouble tonight." Bud scratched his head. "Indians don't attack at night, do they?"

"Not usually," Dakota said, "but we're looking for Jack Rawls and a gang of outlaws to try to rob the train."

"Oh, I didn't know about that." Bud looked very puzzled. "I can't imagine what Rawls expects to find—"

"Just keep your eyes peeled," Dakota said, "or you may get some steel between your shoulder blades."

Bud picked up his Winchester from where it leaned against a wagon wheel. "I'll watch out," he said, and disappeared.

Neither Nora nor Dakota said anything for several minutes. She finished the sock and reached for a bag that lay on the ground beside her. Opening it, she put away her needle, thread, scissors, darning egg, and thimble. She folded the darned sock carefully and laid it on her lap, and then she stared at the fire, her lips squeezed tightly together.

Finally, Dakota said, "I understand you consider me disgusting, Miss Nelson."

"Oh, I do, Mr. Jones. Indeed, I do."

"Well, you just have to make allowances for savages," he said. "We get disgusting once in a while."

"You do," she agreed warmly. "You certainly do."

"Oh hell, Nora!" he said, and with that single roar out of him, he lowered his voice. "There wasn't any danger last night, camped right beside the fort the way we were. I ran into a couple of friends, and we had a drink or two too many. Is there anything wrong with that?"

"There certainly is! I don't care to see any man get into a condition where he is not responsible for what he does, and you were in that condition last night. You—you even insisted on singing, and the song was not a nice one."

"Aw. I didn't realize I did anything as bad as that. I apologize, Nora."

"An apology does not alter the facts," she said sternly. "It's bad enough to see any man drunk, but when it's a man you—you—"

"A man you like?" he suggested.

"I did not say that," she said quickly. "I don't like you now. Not one bit. I don't like the friends you brought with you, either. You're all savages.

I guess it just comes from being with Indians as much as you have."

"You consider Indians more savage than white people?" he asked.

"Of course."

He looked at her in the thinning twilight that was close to darkness now and decided that she had forgotten too much too soon.

"Nora, do you know how the Raw Hide Buttes got their name?"

"I do not," she said, "and I'm sure I wouldn't be the least bit interested."

"I think you would," he said. "I'm going to tell you anyway because it's a good story. It happened a long time ago, back during the gold rush to California. Some young white fellow said he was going to shoot the first Indian he saw crossing the plains. This was before they started, somewhere along the Mississippi. He didn't see any Indians until they got here. There was a camp yonder along the creek, and somebody reminded this young fool about the statement he'd made, so he picked up his rifle and shot the first Indian he could draw a bead on.

"There wasn't any reason for him to murder the Indian—they were behaving themselves all right—but he killed a young brave just the same. The Indians came to the white camp and wanted the man who'd done the shooting. They outnumbered the whites, and I guess the whites didn't have much sympathy for the fool who'd done the killing. So they turned him over to the Indians, and the Indians took him and skinned him alive right out where the whites could see it. I guess they heard him screaming bloody murder for a long time before he died. That's why these buttes and the creek here are called Raw Hide."

She shuddered. "How horrible."

"It sure was," he agreed. "It's like most of the trouble with the Indians. Some fool white man does a stupid thing like shooting down a peaceful Indian in cold blood, and then we wonder why we have trouble with them."

"I meant skinning him alive!" she said sharply. "That's what was horrible."

"He had it coming," Dakota said. "For him to just stand here and shoot—"

"You mean to tell me that you consider it more horrible to shoot somebody than to torture him to death by skinning him alive?"

"Sure," Dakota said. "You expect something like that from an Indian, but a white man is supposed to be civilized."

"Oh, you are a savage," she breathed. "You are a detestable, insufferable savage." She got up and disappeared into the wagon.

Dakota walked back to Barney Ryan's camp. Ryan said, "The moth—"

"Shut up," Dakota said. "I'm going to sleep."

But he didn't drop off easily this night. The

camp became silent except for the pacing of the guards. The sky was very clear with countless stars, and since there was no moon, the stars seemed brighter than usual.

Dakota couldn't quit thinking, no matter how hard he tried. Finally, he got up, stepped outside the wagon circle, and moved around it. Jubal had assigned four guards to the first shift. Dakota met them one after the other, all a little nervous and all glad to see him and talk a minute.

When he came to Bud Nelson, the boy asked, "How'd you make out with Sis?"

"Not good," Dakota said.

"Well, she'll get over it. Give her a little time."

"I don't know why I should," Dakota growled and walked on.

Dakota returned to the Ryan wagon, and this time he did sleep. But he woke before dawn, and the thinking took up where it had left off, and after a while it reached the point where he had to get up and get moving.

Again, he started around the wagon circle.

He met one guard who said everything was quiet. He passed the tent and the surrey, and a moment later reached the supply wagon. He stopped, his right hand instinctively falling to the handle of his knife, and an instant later yells and gunfire broke out on the far side of the circle.

His first impulse was to head for the commotion, but he checked it. Abby had said the gold was in the supply wagon. The big hullabaloo might be a scheme to draw everybody over to the far side of camp.

Jubal Burke began shouting orders, and then Tubal's voice was added to Jubal's. Women screamed, and children began to cry. Dakota, pressed against the back wheel of the supply wagon, glimpsed a movement in the darkness. Something was wriggling along the ground toward the circle. It had to be a man. Yep. A man was worming his way toward the supply wagon.

Dakota wanted to draw his gun and start shooting, but he didn't. It was too easy to miss in the darkness. Besides, he wanted to know who the fellow was. So he waited while the racket on the far side of the circle got louder and louder.

Suddenly, when the man was not more than ten feet from the wagon, he came up off the ground and lunged toward it. He put a foot on the hub of the front wheel and had almost pulled himself up when Dakota reached him. Dakota grabbed an arm and yanked the man off the wheel with his left hand. His right hand drove the knife into the man's back.

The outlaw screamed. A second man materialized out of the darkness. A knife slashed at Dakota. He wheeled away, letting the first man fall, his blade still buried in backbone. He saw the flash of starshine on bright steel and knew he had to give ground until the fellow made a mistake. He backpedaled, stumbled over a chunk, and fell backward. He glimpsed the shadowy form rushing at him, and he doubled his knees and kicked hard with both feet. The resulting thump felt mighty good.

The knife man flipped backwards and was slow getting up. Dakota got his feet under him, drew his gun, and fired twice. He heard the *chunk* of his second bullet striking solid flesh and saw the man go down again.

Backing up, Dakota held his cocked gun in his right hand, but the man didn't move. Presently, the shooting and yelling from the opposite side of the wagon circle died down, and Jubal shouted, "They're pulling out. Looks like they got a bellyful."

Still, Dakota remained motionless beside the supply wagon until the Burke twins, Malone, Ballard, Hargadine, and several other men appeared.

"Get a lantern," Dakota said. "I think I've got a couple of dead men here."

Hargadine tripped over one of the bodies and cursed and moved back. A moment later, Abby appeared with a lighted lantern. Dakota took it and held it over the man he'd shot. It was Hemp Childers. He was dead, the bullet having caught him in the chest. Dakota moved forward to the second man. This one was Summers, and his face had been pounded into one great purple bruise.

Dakota reached down and yanked the knife

out of Summers's back. He said, "I whipped this man, but I didn't do that to his face."

"I'd say Rawls done it," Jubal said, "as punishment for spilling his guts. Somebody must have held Summers's hands behind him while Rawls worked him over."

"Get some shovels," Hargadine said. "We'll have to bury these men."

Dakota waited until he had a chance to see Hargadine alone. Then he said, "The only place they were serious about getting into was the supply wagon. All the yelling and shooting was on the other side. And the trick might have worked if I hadn't been here."

Hargadine stared at Dakota in the thin dawn light.

"Well?" he said finally.

"I know about the gold," Dakota said. "It's hid in a barrel of flour in the supply wagon. But how did *they* know?"

"Good question," Hargadine said. "I wish I could answer it."

Chapter 19

The wagon train was an hour later than usual pulling out of camp that morning. Just as Dakota mounted, Nora walked toward him, her head held high.

"Dakota, wait."

He obeyed, thinking she was probably going to cut him down another notch because he had killed two men before breakfast. When she reached him, she said, "I want to apologize for what I said last night."

"Well," Dakota said, "I—uh—"

"I'm glad you *are* a little bit of a savage, Mr. Jones. Bud told me what happened this morning."

Dakota swallowed a large lump that had formed in his throat. This was some girl. She was stubborn and proud and ornery and honest, and she had spunk, and everything she said had to be listened to very carefully because you never could be sure what was coming next. The man who married her would really have himself a first-rate interesting girl, if he didn't strangle her first.

"Thank you," he said, "ma'am. And I am sorry, too, about getting drunk and singing that dirty song. I never could carry a tune anyhow."

She relaxed visibly and even smiled a little.

"Come see us tonight after supper, Mr. Jones."

"I sure will," he said.

He joined Malone and Ballard, who were mounted and waiting for Jubal to signal the train into motion. Malone said, "You want to tell me what Hargadine's got in that one wagon those bastards wanted so bad?"

"Whisky, maybe," Dakota suggested.

"Whisky, hell," Ballard said in a low tone. "They wouldn't risk tackling an outfit this big for whisky. Not when there was only about seven of 'em." He shook his head. "You're gonna have to do better'n that, Dakota."

"Maybe he's carrying some gold," Dakota said in an offhand way, "though you'd think gold would be coming out of the Hills instead of going in."

"You would for a fact," Malone said, "but gold will draw outlaws just like honey draws bees. It'll work every time."

"You're guessing there were only five men who started the ball?" Dakota asked.

"That's what I'm guessing," Malone nodded. "They were out there in the grass quite a ways, but we could count the rifles."

"You figure any of them got hit?"

"One mebbe," Malone said. "By the time they pulled back, only four rifles was working."

Jubal rode up with Hargadine then. Abby was in the surrey, the lines in her hands. Dakota said,

"We'll stop at Running Water tonight. It's only fifteen miles, but it's too far to go on to Sage Creek."

"We'll be there," Jubal said.

Hargadine nodded, his face still showing strain. Dakota rode northwest for a short distance, then swung north, keeping the Raw Hide Buttes to the west. Malone and Ballard stayed within sight of the train all day, riding on the flanks, and Dakota tried to do the same from his position in front, although there were times when intervening ridges blocked his view.

Dakota seldom played hunches, but he had one today that he couldn't get rid of. He had a feeling that every time he reached the crest of the ridge, he would see a band of Indians below him.

The Red Cloud Agency was directly east of him and not far on the other side of the Nebraska line, so today's and probably tomorrow's journey would take the wagon train directly across the route of travel that was most likely to be used by Indian bands that were trying to get back to the agency after the battle on the Rosebud.

But the day was a peaceful one. Hotter than the past days had been, almost sultry, with a wind that dried a man's skin and cracked his lips. A few white clouds that piled up on the western horizon began to turn dark by noon. Thunder made an ominous roar that at the time seemed to be no more than an empty threat.

The train pulled into Running Water late in the afternoon and corralled.

"See anything?" Dakota asked his flankers.

"Horsebackers," said Malone, who had been west of the wagons. "White men. Four of 'em, but they sure kept their distance."

Ballard hadn't even seen that much. A number of men on horses and some in light rigs had passed the wagon train. A stagecoach had gone past, too, but there had been nothing which seemed to promise trouble.

At supper, Barney Ryan commented on Dakota's unusual restlessness.

"What do you smell in the air?" he asked. "Outlaws or Indians?"

"Neither one, Barney," Dakota said, "though I'll admit I'm a mite edgy." He raised his face toward the sky, half-covered by sullen, black clouds. "We're going to get a storm before morning. A bad one would play hell with the road. It might make us lose a day."

He filled and lighted his pipe and got up.

"I'm going to see if the flame will consume the moth," he said. "It sure come close last night."

Halfway to the Nelson wagon, he heard someone yell on the other side of the circle. Nora and Bud joined him, and they waited and watched together. A rider was coming in fast from the west. A soldier.

Dakota and the Nelsons ran toward the Hargadine tent. Jubal and Tubal went to meet the soldier. By the time all the people in camp gathered at the Hargadine tent, the Burke twins had brought the soldier in and helped him out of the saddle. He was dirty and so tired that he had trouble keeping his legs from folding under him.

Bruce Bascom stepped forward and took the reins. "I'll tend to your horse, soldier," he said.

The courier was hardly more than a boy, probably nineteen, Dakota guessed.

"Thank you, all," he said hoarsely. "If I could have a cup of coffee, I'd feel better. I've come a ways today."

"Sure, you can," Jubal said. Turning, he called, "How about it, ladies?"

Mrs. Bascom poured coffee into a tin cup and handed it to the soldier while Abby sliced bacon into a frying pan. The soldier's hands trembled as he reached for the cup. He drained it and handed it back and Mrs. Bascom filled it again.

"It hits the spot," he said.

He drank more slowly this time, glancing around at the people surrounding him.

"Where you headed, soldier?" Dakota asked.

"Fort Robinson, sir. I've got some dispatches to deliver telling about the Custer fight." He finished the coffee and wiped a hand across his mouth. "I guess you folks haven't heard about it."

"No," Hargadine said. "We haven't heard anything."

"He got wiped out on the Little Bighorn," the courier said. "Five whole companies of the Seventh Cavalry. Some other companies survived. Seems he divided his command, and the troops under Reno and Benteen held out. But the Indians killed Custer and all of the officers and men who were with him."

For a long time, no one spoke. Dakota, knowing Custer better than anyone in camp, was not so surprised as the rest, but he did reflect wryly about his conversation with Captain Monroe at Fort Laramie.

Monroe had said the Indians were too individualistic, that they would scatter after the Rosebud fight. Well, they hadn't. Actually, more warriors must have gathered. It took a lot of braves to wipe out five companies of the Seventh. Custer was a fighter, if nothing else.

Abby said, "Here's your supper, soldier."

He took the tin plate and ate standing up. Bascom had watered his horse and brought him back. He asked, "What's happened?" His wife told him as he stripped off the saddle and rubbed the animal down. Bascom sighed and said, "I guess a man orders the events of his life."

"What do you mean by that?" somebody asked. "You think Custer committed suicide?"

"In a sense, yes," Bascom said.

They jeered at him until Dakota, thinking of Custer's way of doing things, said, "He's right." After that, no one said any more about it.

The soldier finished his meal and drank another cup of coffee, then said, "I've got to keep moving. Watch out for Indians tomorrow. The country I just came through is crawling with 'em, all moving this way."

He left, riding east toward Fort Robinson. The people returned to their wagons, still subdued by the news. Bruce Bascom, walking beside Dakota but practically running to keep up stride, said, "You were the only one who understood what I meant."

"I was with Custer two years ago," Dakota said, "so I knew him."

"I have read about him," Bascom said, "but what I meant was, there are no accidents. We determine what will happen to us by how we live and what we think."

Dakota nodded absently. Tomorrow they would see Indians. He had never been more certain of anything in his life.

Chapter 20

The thunder rumbled all night, coming louder and closer toward morning. A hard wind sprang up, bringing with it the smell of rain and dropping the temperature by at least twenty degrees. The lightning was brilliant and frightening, lashing down at a trembling earth from the black clouds, and for that one instant, each flash made the camp as bright as day.

Just at dawn, the storm struck with devastating fury. Although the actual rain did not last more than fifteen minutes, the result was worse than that which would have followed an ordinary rain lasting all day. It was a scary quarter of an hour, with lightning bouncing around very close and the prospect of a flash flood pouring down the valley.

The tent went down with the first savage gust. Abby's, Janie's, and Sweet Betsy's screams almost drowned out the thunder until Jubal and Tubal Burke got them out from under the wet canvas and into the wagon. Even then, they were soaked to the skin. The guards and anyone who had been sleeping outside crawled into wagons, but by the time the storm moved on east, everyone in camp was more or less wet.

Dakota went first to the Nelson wagon, calling, "Nora! Bud! You all right?"

Nora poked her head out. "Right as rain, Dakota."

"Oh, you are funny," he said. "That wasn't a rain. Somebody up yonder kicked the bucket over."

"Whatever He kicked," Nora said brightly, "it sure was brimful."

Dakota went on to the Bascom wagon.

The Bascoms were all right, Mrs. Bascom singing out with her usual vigor. The Akers and Starbuck women were almost hysterical, the children crying, and the men "cold, wet, and hungry, damn it."

Dakota went on to the "joy wagon," which held no joy at all this morning, what with Sweet Betsy crying softly and Janie cursing her way through an astonishing vocabulary learned from many lovers. But Abby said, "Oh, sure, we're all right. Why in hell we left the comforts of civilization for this I'll never know—but we're all right."

Jubal crawled out of the wagon, Tubal following.

"I never seen a worse one," Jubal said.

"Me neither," Tubal said.

"What will this do to the road?" Jubal asked.

"We may have to sit here all day," Dakota said. "Or at least till the water goes down in the ravines."

"Sam will bust his buttons," Jubal said. "He's

been scared ever since our fight yesterday morning. He's beginning to think that maybe Duke Wynne didn't give it to him straight about when Elling was leaving Sidney."

"He's slow," Abby said bitterly, "but he finally learns."

"The thing is, he don't want to lose any time," Jubal said, "just in case Elling has got ahead of him."

"We didn't order the storm," Dakota said, "though it seems to me you guaranteed good weather all the way to Deadwood."

"Yeah, you done so, Jubal," Tubal said. "How about it?"

"This is good weather," Jubal said. "It'll make the grass grow. Pass that dry wood out to me, Tubal. I'll start a fire if I can find a place that ain't drowned."

"You won't find any such place this morning," Dakota said.

He went on to the supply wagon, where he found Hargadine crouched in the back, his revolver in his hand.

"You won't get robbed this morning," Dakota said.

"No, I guess not, but I got to thinking that the storm would have been a good time to sneak up and steal my dinero and vamoose." Hargadine stepped to the ground and sank to his ankles in the mud. "Damn storm. What can we do, Jones?

I don't want to sit here and lose a whole day's travel."

"I'm going to saddle up and ride ahead for a mile or two," Dakota said. "No use to start until the middle of the morning. This time of year, the sky will likely clear off, the sun will shine, and by noon, it'll be hot. The ground will be fairly solid except in the ruts and holes. The big thing is that, if the storm was bad west of here, we'll find the ravines running bank full. If that's the case, there's nothing to do but wait till the water goes down."

"We can't," Hargadine said, tight-lipped. "We've got to keep moving."

"Then you'll be moving downstream," Dakota said, irritated by the man's irrational stubbornness. "There is one possibility. These storms are spotty. Sometimes you get a gully washer where you are, and half a mile from where you're standing, it hasn't even rained. We'll have to find out."

Dakota went on. Dogface Malone and Squint Ballard came toward him, gingerly stepping around the ankle-deep puddles of water.

"Saddle up," Dakota said. "We're riding north a piece to see how things look."

A few minutes later, Dakota and his flankers rode out of camp. The sky was clear. The rainstorm had moved east, the lightning still visible, the thunder gradually becoming more distant.

Later, the sun tipped up over the horizon, a blazing arc that grew in size until the entire circle showed blinding red above the line of storm clouds.

For the first half mile, the footing was treacherous, but the ground sloped, and the water had drained off, so it would soon be dry. Then the land tipped down the next mile to a ravine. When they reached it, Dakota saw exactly what he had expected: a flood of chocolate-brown water reaching almost to the top of both banks. The current was swift, digging away at the south bank. The wagons would have trouble when they tried to cross.

"It'll go down as it came up," Malone said. "Time we go back and eat breakfast, and the wagons get here, the bottom of that ravine will be nothing but mud."

"Which will make it a son of a bitch to pull a heavy wagon through," Dakota said.

"I'm glad it ain't our worry," Ballard said. "The teamsters can have the job of driving them long-eared bastards. I don't want it."

They turned back, Dakota scanning the ridge tops on both sides of the valley and then looking up and down the valley itself. The country was empty. He could see nothing moving.

When they reached the wagons, most of the water had drained off, but it was still a soaked and bedraggled camp, blue smoke from the cook fires rising into the cold, damp air of early morning.

Dakota reined to a stop at the tent, which had been put up again. Jubal was fussing with a fire that stubbornly gave out more smoke than flames. Apparently, he hadn't had enough dry wood to get a good fire going.

Abby stood beside Jubal, shaking her head in disgust. Janie was crouched behind her, pale and shivering, the collar of her wet coat pulled up under her chin. She'd be warmer without it, but Dakota had no intention of telling her.

He liked Abby, and he could stand Sweet Betsy, but to him Janie was a cold-blooded, conniving little tart who would cut your throat for a dime. Why Hargadine had trusted her was more than Dakota could understand. The man prided himself on his knowledge of human nature, and it struck Dakota that at least fifty percent of his judgments had been wrong.

Dakota rode on, deciding that he wouldn't try to talk to Jubal until he had his coffee at least. Barney Ryan had been more farsighted than most in the train: he had kept an ample supply of dry wood in his wagon. He started cooking breakfast as soon as he saw Dakota, and when Dakota dismounted, Ryan gave him an armload of dry wood.

"I'm a worrier," Ryan said. "Whenever I had a chance to pick up some wood, I did it, so I've got plenty. You take that to Nora, and she'll love you even more than she does now."

"That's possible," Dakota said. "Barely possible."

Dakota dropped the dry wood noisily beside Nora's smoldering fire.

"I told Bud this would happen," she raged. "It wasn't sensible to think we'd go all the way to Deadwood without running into a storm, but Bud never got around to saving more than a few sticks, so this morning he has to rustle a batch of wet wood that won't even boil water, but you can bet he wants his breakfast."

Dakota tapped her on the shoulder and pointed downward.

"This dry wood is sent with the compliments of Mr. Barney Ryan," he said. "Your brother, Bud, is nowhere in sight, but Mr. Ryan's dry wood is."

Nora Nelson looked down. She blushed, she bit her lips, and then she began to giggle.

"Please thank Mr. Barney Ryan," she said. "Like this."

She kissed Dakota on the cheek, then backed away, blushing further.

"I'll thank him," Dakota said, "but not, by God, like that."

Shortly after breakfast, Dakota rode back to the tent where Hargadine stood talking to the Burke twins. Dakota said, "By the time everybody has finished eating and gets hooked up, I think you can travel. There's a ravine over the next ridge that was running bank full, but the water will go down in a hurry. The trouble is, the current has cut the south bank away, so you'll have to get some men to shovel it down a little."

"I suppose we'll have to double-team to get across the gully," Jubal said, and Tubal added in disgust, "We'll be all day crossing it. The mud will be ten feet deep in the bottom."

"Maybe only nine." Dakota glanced at Abby, who was just finishing cooking breakfast, and lowered his voice. "Watch out for hostiles. This is the day, so don't get so interested crossing that ravine that they surprise you."

"Where are you going to be?" Jubal demanded.

"Around."

"How do you know this is the day?" Hargadine demanded nervously.

"I'm a hunch player," Dakota said.

He rode toward Malone and Ballard. They finished eating as he came up, dropped their tin plates and cups into the wreck pan, and wiped their mouths with the backs of their hands.

"We're ready," Malone said.

They rode north a few minutes later, the horses' hoofs making sucking sounds in the mud. Dakota said, "They'll be till noon getting across that ravine. We'll do well to make it to Sage Creek by dark."

"It's only twelve miles, ain't it?" Ballard said.

"That's right, but we won't be rolling all afternoon. We'll be fighting off Indians part of the time."

"You're mighty sure of it," Malone said.

"He's got a right to be," Ballard said, "because that's what's going to happen. I can smell 'em from here." He hipped around in the saddle, looked back at the camp and up and down the valley, then turned to Dakota. "How are we going to do this? If they hit the wagons while they're crossing the ravine, there'll be hell to pay."

Dakota nodded. He had thought of that. If the train was caught with half the wagons on each side of the ravine, it would be impossible to corral, and the Indians could chew up each half, one at a time.

"I'm going to ride on ahead a little farther than I have been doing," Dakota said. "Squint, you circle back and ride to the top of the ridge south of the valley. Dogface, you move on west along this ridge. Go as far as you think you can safely."

Malone scowled. "It ain't smart for any of us to get too far from the wagons—just in case you're guessing right about this being the day."

"If it ain't the day," Ballard said, "I figure the odds are that we'll make it to Deadwood without seeing an Indian."

"That's my guess, too," Dakota said. "So it's really a matter of judgment. All I can say is, don't take chances. My notion was to cover as big an area as possible so we could give the word that the Indians were around and let Jubal have more time to get the wagons into a circle."

They separated, Dakota riding north. When he reached the ravine, he found that the water was down to a mere trickle. Still, the wagons would have to double-team because of the mud. He put his sorrel across the bottom, the horse laboring until he reached solid footing on the other side. Dakota shook his head as he climbed to the top of the north bank. It would take the morning and then some to get all the wagons across.

He rode to the top of the ridge and pulled up. He studied the country to the west, broken by numerous ravines similar to the one behind him. There was some scattered timber here, but it wasn't thick enough to hide a band of Indians. He could see a long way to the west, and there was another ridge to the north and probably another one beyond that. The truth was, half the Sioux nation could hide between these ridges, and he wouldn't see them until they wanted to be seen, or until he topped the ridge above them.

He dismounted, filled and lighted his pipe, and waited. Presently, Jubal Burke and Hargadine rode over the ridge to the south. Then came the surrey, and after it the wagons broke over the crest and began to roll downhill.

When Jubal and Hargadine reached the ravine, Jubal got down and inspected the south bank.

When Tubal arrived with the "joy wagon," Jubal met him and took out two shovels. They began to work, making a slope that the wagons could negotiate. Presently, other men joined with more shovels, and in a few minutes, the bank had been sloped all the way to the bottom of the ravine.

Hargadine came across and rode up the ridge to where Dakota stood beside his sorrel. Hargadine dismounted and asked, "What do you think now?"

"I'm thinking we better get every wagon across that ravine in a hurry," Dakota said. "We'll be in trouble if the Indians show up with only half the wagons on this side."

Hargadine studied the broken country to the west, then looked north to the next ridge.

"This country is all ridges and hollows," he complained. "They could be right over there, and we wouldn't know it."

"That's right," Dakota said. "I just naturally figured they would come from the west and be headed east to the Red Cloud Agency. Now I'm not so sure. They could come down from the north like you said."

Neither talked after that. Hargadine lit a cigar and watched moodily as the wagons below him crossed the ravine, the mules laboring through the mud. It took a long time, as Dakota had known it would, what with the moving of teams back and forth, and the hooking up and unhooking.

None of the wagons stuck in the mud, however. Shortly after noon, they were all across and climbing the slope below Dakota.

"I'm going to ride north and see if there is anything on the other side of the next ridge," Dakota said. "You go back and tell Jubal not to take time to eat. We can make it on two meals today."

Hargadine nodded and rode back. Dakota reined his sorrel around and rode down the long slant. He reached the bottom and glanced up at the crest of the next ridge. In that exact instant, the Indians broke over the top. They sounded like a hundred yelling devils, Dakota thought as he whirled his horse and started back the way he had come.

Several of the braves in front began to fire. Bullets smacked the ground behind the sorrel. They'd be in range if they gained on him just a little, and the chances were he'd be a dead man.

They looked like devils, too, he thought as he glanced over his shoulder. They were painted and completely naked except for their moccasins, breech clouts, and headgear made of feathers and horns. The thought ran through his mind that these warriors were just as savage as Nora Nelson considered them, a fact they would demonstrate firsthand if they captured him. He wondered what Nora would say if she saw his body afterward.

He leaned low in his saddle to make as small

a target as he could. The sorrel had brought him through more than one chase like this, but he was going uphill over muddy ground. Even though the horse was shod, he was slipping with every lunging step.

Dakota looked up at the crest of the ridge. It didn't seem to be getting much closer. When he glanced back over his shoulder a second time, his heart felt as if it had dropped below his stomach. The lead warriors were close, much closer than he had expected, and certainly within rifle range. Even as he looked back at them, the two in front raised their guns to fire.

Chapter 21

Dakota reined up, yanked his rifle from the scabbard, dismounted, and dropped to one knee.

The two braves in front had obviously not expected him to make a stand. Surprised, they held their fire for a moment; then, when they did shoot, both missed by two feet. They didn't get another chance.

Dakota's first shot took the Indian on his left out of his saddle in a rolling fall. The horse turned at a sharp angle and kept on running. The second Indian pulled his paint pony to a stop. The paint reared and fought his rider for a moment, defeating whatever plan the brave had. The pony bucked and plunged so that Dakota had to wait a few seconds. Then the animal swung sideways, and Dakota shot the Indian through the head. He threw up his hands and spilled to the ground.

Quickly, Dakota stepped into the saddle and put the sorrel on up the slope again. He had lost a few seconds, but he had slowed the mass of the Indians. None of the warriors wanted to get any closer to a man who could shoot like that.

A moment later, someone started firing from the crest of the ridge. The Indians split into two groups that swerved outward, bent on taking the ridge from the flanks.

When Dakota reached the crest, he saw Hargadine lying on his stomach, firing with a rifle as fast as he could lever shells into the chamber and pull the trigger.

"Get back to the wagons!" Dakota yelled as he raced past the gambler. He took off his hat and waved it as he shouted, "Corral! Corral!"

But Jubal had already started to turn the surrey and the lead wagons. Still, it seemed to take a long time. Dakota came flying down the hill, the sorrel kicking up gobs of mud behind him. He glanced back once and saw Hargadine on his black horse, racing toward the wagons. Malone and Ballard were coming, too.

Now the wagon train was curling like a great snake. By the time Dakota reached it, the circle was complete. The drivers were on the ground, unhooking the horses and mules and turning them into a circle when the Indians came over the hill.

Dakota gained the wagon corral a moment later. He stepped out of leather, pulled his rifle from the scabbard, and yelled, "Stay down. Start shooting. Don't let 'em overrun us."

Then Hargadine was inside. Malone and Ballard pounded in. Teamsters and settlers dropped to the ground behind the wheels of the wagons and began shooting. Rifle fire made a continuous, crackling sputter.

The Indians were still split into two bands, but

both bands charged straight at the train. Dakota dropped down next to Nora. She was kneeling beside the front wheel of her wagon and firing as steadily as Bud.

"Get down!" he yelled at her. "Flat on your belly. Stick your face down into the dirt."

She yelled back, "I can shoot, too, damn it. How do you expect me to shoot with my face in the dirt?"

Dakota was too busy firing to argue with her.

Half a dozen ponies galloped away, riderless. The bodies of the braves who had been on them a moment ago lay motionless in the grass. Suddenly, the Indians lost interest in overrunning the whites. They turned sharply and began circling, each brave clinging to the offside of his pony so that very little of his brown body was exposed while he snapped off shots under the pony's neck.

They were yelling like maniacs and keeping up a steady fire that wasn't accurate but served to keep the whites pinned to the ground. Inside the wagon circle, the horses and mules were plunging and kicking. Several mules were down, and others had been hit.

Janie was screaming in terror, and Sweet Betsy lay belly-flat in the mud. Abby had piled several boxes of rifle shells in front of her and was loading the rifles and passing them back to Hargadine and the Burke twins. Mrs. Bascom was loading, too, keeping one rifle until her small husband emptied the other gun, and then exchanging with him.

The Akers and Starbuck women and children were staying down, and it seemed to Dakota that neither Ira Starbuck nor Len Akers was doing his proper share of shooting. Everybody else was, though, and Dakota, taking time to glance around, felt an impulse to stand up and cheer.

Indian ponies were being shot down, plunging and kicking and rolling, their riders trying to crawl away from the devastating fire. Some of the braves didn't crawl fast enough, and many lay motionless in the grass.

Dakota was not surprised when, a few minutes later, the Indians gathered their dead and wounded and streamed back up the hill, stopping only when they were out of rifle range. Then the defenders stood up and cheered.

Bruce Bascom waved his rifle in one hand and his hat in the other as he jumped up and yelled louder than anyone else. Mrs. Bascom, slapping him on the back so hard she almost knocked him down, bellowed, "You did it, Hercules! You drove them off!"

Ira Starbuck wheeled on her, snarling, "You're a fool, woman. Your little runt couldn't—"

Len Akers grabbed his friend by an arm, hissing in his ear, "Shut up, Ira! Shut up!"

Dakota frowned, only half listening. He was watching Nora, who stood a few feet from him, patting her rifle fondly. Her hair was all tangled, and she had a blob of drying mud alongside her nose, and she looked so beautiful it was a crime.

"There go your savages, Mr. Jones!" she yelled at him. "Looks to me like us white people are better fighters than they are."

Dakota walked over and stopped one step from her. "You're forgetting there were some savages among us white people, Miss Nelson."

"And who would that be, Mr. Jones?"

"Me," Dakota said, shoving his face forward so that the end of his nose was within an inch of the end of hers. "Also, Malone and Ballard. And another thing. Why can't you let the men do the fighting? Don't you know you're a woman?"

"You bet I know I'm a woman!" she shouted. "I can shoot as straight as any man here, including you. Don't try cutting me down to size, Mr. Jones!"

For a few seconds, they glared at each other, faces almost touching, and then Bud said, "Why don't you kiss her, Dakota? Can't you see she's aching for it?"

Dakota's first impulse was to turn around and slap some respect into Bud; then he decided that a good kissing would serve her right. He wrapped an arm around her and pulled her to him and kissed her hard and thoroughly. She swelled up fit to bust when he let her go. She'd been insulted, of course, and she heard some of the people laugh, and when Barney Ryan said, "That's the best way to end a fight," he only made it worse.

She said, "You have just confirmed my original opinion, Mr. Jones. You are first and last and *always* a savage."

Squint Ballard said, "By God, Dakota, I don't see how you can stand such an uppity woman. I'd lodge-pole her for saying that. You're too soft with your women. You always were."

Nora wheeled on him. "I am not *his* woman. Someday, I'm going to—"

"Come on." Ballard jerked his head at Dakota. "Jubal wants you over here."

Dakota followed Squint Ballard.

Jubal and Tubal were standing next to the surrey with Hargadine and several other men. Jubal pointed to the Indians, who had stopped just out of rifle range. The warriors seemed to be carrying on some kind of argument.

"Malone says they're trying to decide whether they ought to hit us again or get out of here," Jubal said. "They don't figure any other whites are going to come along right away after the big storm, so maybe they think it'll pay 'em just to hold us here and take a few shots and wear down our nerves."

Dakota shook his head. "I don't think so. We hurt them pretty bad. I think they'll pull out. It didn't go the way they figured it would."

"I can tell you one thing sure," Malone said.

"If we had a long-range rifle and somebody who could shoot it, we could knock one of them red bastards off his horse. That'd make up their minds for 'em mighty damn quick."

"We don't have one," Hargadine said. "I'd have bought one in Cheyenne if I'd known we'd need it, but no one told me."

Bruce Bascom tugged at the fringe on Dakota's sleeve. "I've got one in my wagon," he said in an apologetic tone as if he thought everybody would wonder why he had it. "A Sharps. It's a good rifle, a real good rifle."

"You're dreaming," Jubal said. "Why, them Injuns are damn near half a mile away. You couldn't even shoot that far, let alone hit one of 'em."

Bascom looked at him for a moment, then he said mildly, "I can shoot that far and I can hit one of them. It's a Sharps .50 buffalo gun."

"Get it," Dakota said.

Bascom ran to his wagon. He came back cradling a huge rifle that seemed too much for him to handle. It had a short telescope and Dakota guessed that it weighed twelve to fifteen pounds.

No one said a word as Bascom walked to the back wheel of the supply wagon and rested the heavy weapon on top of the wheel.

"Now, gentlemen," he said, "if you will tell me which Indian you want shot, I will shoot him."

Jubal muttered, "My God," and put a hand to his forehead.

Malone and Ballard looked at Dakota. Dakota shrugged. Then Malone said with a straight face, "See that big one on the paint pony? He's off to the left and a little apart from most of 'em. I seen him while ago when they was circling us and I thought he was Big Bear. If he is, he's the one giving most of the orders. If you knock him over, they'll hightail out of here."

"All right," Bascom said, "I'll shoot him."

"I'm dreaming," Jubal said. "This ain't happening."

"Of course not," Tubal said. "You're still in school and Bascom's sitting behind you with a pea shooter and—"

"Shut up," Hargadine said. "Give him a chance, at least."

The little man ignored them. He fired twice to get his range, then settled down and sighted carefully. The seconds piled up. The scoffers stopped breathing. Then Bascom pulled the trigger, and the Sharps again made its reverberating, booming sound. A great cloud of smoke rolled out of the muzzle and slowly plumed into the damp air. Big Bear pitched out of his saddle as if lightning had struck him.

A sigh went up in the wagon corral.

"I still don't believe it," Jubal said.

Then they cheered. They hammered Bascom

on the back and told him what a tremendous shot he'd made. He smiled as if he had not done anything great at all and staggered back to his wagon under the weight of the Sharps.

Mrs. Bascom took the gun from him and laid it in the wagon, and then she enfolded him in her huge arms and almost smothered him with kisses. After she released him, she said, "You are wonderful, Hercules. You are simply wonderful."

She was more than half right, Dakota thought, watching the Indians. They did a lot of confused, excited milling around, and then they picked up Big Bear and carried him away. The tailenders disappeared over the ridge, and that was the last of them.

"They never will understand what happened," Jubal said, almost sadly. "They just ain't used to bolts from heaven."

Dakota chuckled dryly. "Are we hurt any, Jubal?"

"Not much," Jubal said. "Two mules dead and a couple of other ones hit purty bad. I guess we'll have to shoot 'em. One teamster got a bullet hole in his left arm. I guess he was the only one hit. Oh yes, Janie got her dress muddy."

Nobody smiled. For the first time Dakota realized he was not alone in his feeling about the woman. He said to Hargadine, "I'm riding to the top of the hill and see if they've gone. Get hooked up, but don't move until you see me wave."

Hargadine nodded. Dakota ran to his sorrel, slid his rifle into the boot, tightened the cinch, and stepped up. Minutes later, he was on the ridge, studying the country, and waved his hat. The surrey started up the hill, and the big circle began to unwind.

They reached Sage Creek at dusk, tired and dirty and very hungry, but no one felt like complaining.

"We got out of that one pretty lucky," Abby said, and that summed it up for everybody.

Chapter 22

They turned west the following morning, making only fifteen miles that day. The rain had not struck here, and they were in dust again and hot weather. That evening, Nora told Dakota she didn't know which was worse, to get wet and cold and have to travel through mud, or to breathe and eat dust while the sun burned your skin until you hurt.

She didn't hold the kiss against him, Dakota thought, but, well, to hell with her. Ballard had said it: She needed a good lodge-poling. He didn't like an uppity woman, either.

Then he laughed at himself, knowing he didn't mean any of it. Nora Nelson might be stubborn and willful and just plain ornery, but he had never met a more blood-rousing gal in his life.

The next day, they made it to the Cheyenne River. Now the Black Hills made dark bulges against the sky, and a wave of optimism spread through the train. They were almost there.

That night, Dakota hunkered beside the fire in front of the tent, Hargadine and Jubal across from him. Somehow, Abby had cleaned up the gambler's clothes so that he looked as dudish as ever. Hargadine didn't appreciate Abby, that was for sure. But if he preferred a selfish little bitch like Janie, it was his affair, not Dakota's.

"We're not out of Indian country," Dakota told Jubal. "It's my guess that tomorrow will decide it for us. That ten miles through Red Canyon is a bastard. I'll ride ahead, and I'll put Malone and Ballard on the rims, but you'll have to keep your eyes peeled, and everybody in the outfit has got to be ready for trouble."

"Fair enough," Jubal said. "We've gone through too much to be stopped now."

Hargadine had a cigar clamped in the corner of his mouth. He took it out and knocked off an inch of ash and said, "Something's eating on you, Jones. Is it still Rawls?"

"Well," Dakota said, "I had a notion Rawls and some of his men were with the Indians when they hit us. I didn't see any of them, but he might have had a hand in it, some way."

Hargadine snorted. Now that he could see the Hills, confidence had flowed back into him.

"You've made a bogey man out of Jack Rawls ever since we left Cheyenne," he said. "We'll never see him again. I don't understand how a man with your reputation can be scared of an outlaw like Rawls."

There were times when Dakota felt like beating some sense into the man. But now that he had come this far, he had no intention of losing the thousand dollars Hargadine had promised him. He'd go the rest of the way to Deadwood.

To make sure he didn't spoil it, he stood up and walked away.

Next day, they nooned at the mouth of Red Canyon and within an hour started through the gorge. Dakota rode half a mile in front of Jubal and Hargadine, his eyes on the narrow opening ahead of him. Only occasionally did he lift his gaze to the rim. Malone and Ballard were up there, pacing the wagon train, and if they spotted anything alarming, they would let him know.

The steep rock wall rose nearly one thousand feet on both sides of the canyon, a canyon so narrow that the sky was no more than a blue slit above Dakota's head. Now and then, he saw prospect holes, giving notice that they were coming into the mining country.

Another day brought them to Custer City. Here, the first discovery of gold had been made on French Creek, but the town was largely deserted now. Bigger strikes had been made farther north.

It was a pleasant site for a town, located in a small valley surrounded by timbered hills, and an equally pleasant place to camp. They were almost at the end of the journey, Deadwood being only fifty miles farther on.

That evening, Dakota sat beside Nora at her wagon, his pipe in his mouth, his long legs stretched out toward the fire. Bud had gone to the other side of the wagon circle to visit Malone and Ballard, and Dakota found to his surprise that neither he nor Nora had any need to make talk.

He was relaxed, perfectly happy just to sit in silence and puff on his pipe. He had known Indian women with whom he could share this kind of silence, but he had never expected to be able to do it with Nora. He thought about mentioning the Indian women to Nora, but then he smiled around his pipestem and said nothing.

Darkness came, and with it the coolness of the higher altitude. The fragrance of pines spiced the air, and then the vagrant breeze blew wood smoke Dakota's way. From somewhere back in the timber, a night bird made a screeching sound. Two horses inside the wagon circle fought briefly with angry snorts and kicks and then were quiet.

"How long will it take us to reach Deadwood?" Nora asked finally. "Three days?"

"That's about it, Nora. We've got some grades to pull. We can't do it in two."

"What will you do after we get to Deadwood?"

"Oh, keep riding, I guess. Malone and Ballard say they're going to stay in Deadwood for a while at least, but I'm not. I'm going to find me a place for a ranch somewhere west of here in Montana or Wyoming. I've known for a long time that my way of life was gone, but I never faced up to it before."

She leaned forward, looking intently at him in the firelight. She said in a tone so low he barely heard her, "Take me with you, Dakota."

For a moment, he thought he hadn't rightly heard what she had said. He scowled at her, telling himself that if he wanted to take her, he would ask her. Asking was for him to do not her. Then he remembered how she had wanted to be kissed, and how she had egged him into doing it, and suddenly he decided she was not only stubborn and willful and ornery, but by God, she was forward, too.

"I guess that wouldn't be a good idea," he said, and got up and walked away.

Later, as he stared at the sky and tried to sleep, he knew he should not have said what he had and that he should not have walked away. It was just that she hadn't acted the way he thought a woman should act, and he'd ended up making another mistake with her. He seemed to have made mistakes all the way north from Cheyenne.

Well, he wasn't used to white women, he told himself. He'd make up with her in the morning.

But in the morning, she refused to speak to him.

"She's just got another mad on," Bud said. "Pay her no never mind."

Dakota mounted his sorrel and rode to the head of the wagon train. He would take Bud's advice. The hell with her. He didn't want anything to do with a woman who could "get a mad on" as quickly and easily as Nora Nelson.

But as he rode north, the wagon train uncurling behind him, he remembered those good minutes of peace beside the fire.

Chapter 23

When they pulled into camp the following afternoon, they were only ten miles from Deadwood. The road from Custer City had been rough and rocky, the grades steep, and at times there had been room for little more than two ruts hanging to the side of a cliff.

On a number of occasions, Dakota had a feeling that the train was being watched from the timber above them, but there had been no trouble. A small band of road agents would tackle a stagecoach or a few wagons, but a train this size might look too tough.

During the morning, the Starbucks and Akers pulled out of line to follow a gulch which held their claims, and about noon, the Bascoms found a small camp which did not have a store. Bruce Bascom said this was the place they were looking for, so the train stopped long enough to unhook Hargadine's mules and hitch up Bascom's team of horses.

Barney Ryan stayed with the train because he didn't see much chance of establishing a school except in a fair-sized town that promised to keep on growing. So far, there weren't many families in the Hills, but by fall, Deadwood would be even larger than it was now, and he was counting on finding enough children to pay him to start a school.

Neither Nora nor Bud said anything, so Dakota assumed the Nelson wagon would stay with the train until they reached Deadwood. Nora still had not spoken to Dakota, and he had not made another effort to speak to her. Maybe he wouldn't even try, he told himself sourly as he stripped gear from the sorrel and led him to the creek.

They'd roll into Deadwood tomorrow afternoon, and he'd draw his wages and shake hands with a few people and ride west. There was plenty of trouble for a man to get into without taking on a female bobcat with red hair. Well, Nora's hair was more auburn than red, but she sure as hell had a red-headed woman's temper. He'd have a lot easier life if he found a squaw. . .

"Dakota."

He was coming back to the wagon after staking out his horse. He looked up to see Jubal running toward him. He had very seldom seen Jubal Burke excited or upset or even nervous. The twins were the kind of men who took life as it came, confident they could lick anything they had to. Dakota guessed that was the reason he liked them as much as he did. The only thing he didn't understand was their loyalty to Sam Hargadine, which made no better sense than Hargadine's loyalty to Duke Wynne.

But Jubal was worked up about something now.

He was white-faced and trembling with anger. When he reached Dakota, he stopped and tried to speak, but he had to swallow and run the tip of his tongue over his lips before he could manage, "Duke Wynne's here."

Dakota took off his hat and rubbed the top of his head. He grinned ruefully.

"My noggin still hurts where he bent his gun barrel over it. I guess I've got something to square up with that rooster."

"Wait." Jubal grabbed his arm. "Don't go off half-cocked, Dakota. This is what me and Tubal and Abby have been waiting for, but we didn't expect him to just ride into camp like this. Sam still don't believe us about Wynne, and we can't figure out a way to prove it to him."

"What's Wynne here for?"

"I don't know yet," Jubal said. "I want you to come over to the tent where they're talking and try to figure it out. We've brought Sam this far. We can't let Jake Elling shoot him to pieces now."

"I don't see why the hell not," Dakota said. "He's a big boy. We've wet-nursed him all the way up the trail. If he wants to commit suicide, why should we stop him?"

Jubal looked at Dakota as if he were a child who had to be reasoned with. He said slowly, "Do you remember that first morning in Cheyenne when you'd had your bath and a haircut, and you were getting your breakfast, and you hadn't seen Sam yet?"

"I remember, all right."

"You'll likewise remember that we told you there were times when Sam had to be taken care of," Jubal went on. "Well, this is one. He's treated me and Tubal fine. We've got the best-paying jobs we ever had, and we don't aim to lose 'em. He's been purty ornery to Abby, but she claims she loves him and she wants him looked after. I don't know what Wynne's up to, but I do know he's a cheating, tricky son of a bitch, so you've got to do something."

"Me? There's nothing I can do."

"Mebbe not. Mebbe so. I dunno. I just want you to come along and see." When Dakota still hesitated, Jubal said pointedly, "You ain't got your dinero yet. You'd better copper your bet."

"That's the first thing you've said that makes sense," Dakota said.

Inside the tent, Tubal was standing beside Hargadine, and Wynne was facing them. Abby was not in sight. Dakota remembered seeing Wynne in the Palace in Cheyenne, now that he had a good look at the man. He was not so tall as Hargadine, but he was very solidly built, and Dakota could understand now why he had gone down and out when Wynne slugged him with a gun barrel.

If Wynne was aware that Dakota had come in, he gave no hint of it. He stood motionless, a cold-eyed man, as neatly dressed as Hargadine, and, like Hargadine, a man who showed very little expression in his face. His smile, Dakota thought, was part of the mask.

"I'm sorry, Sam, but that's how it is," Wynne was saying. "He got to Deadwood ahead of you, and he has his business booming. He claims there isn't enough carriage trade for both of you in a camp this size. He's probably right. Anyhow, he doesn't want you to lose any money. That's why he's making this offer. He'll buy everything you've got for a fair price. All he wants is a signed agreement that you'll stay out of Deadwood."

"So he doesn't want me to lose any money," Hargadine said. "What's the matter with you, Duke? You know he'd like nothing better than for me to lose my shirt."

"Sure, Sam, but he's willing to forget how he feels about you just to keep from having trouble. He figures that, if you don't lose money in the deal, you'll sign the agreement."

"I'd never make an agreement with Jake Elling," Hargadine said. "I'll kill the bastard before I sign anything."

"You won't kill him, Sam." Wynne sighed and shook his head. "That's why I rode out here. I don't want to see you shot in the street, and that's what will happen if you go after him. You'd never in the world get to him. He's got too many gunslingers around him. He wouldn't give you an even break."

For the first time since Dakota had known Hargadine, the man completely lost his aplomb. His hand actually trembled as he threw it out in a gesture of puzzlement.

"I can't understand it, Duke. We made good time. Elling hadn't even started when I got your wire at Fort Laramie. How could he have beaten us up here?"

"He traveled light, and he had no trouble with weather or Indians or outlaws." Wynne paused, and then he said coldly, "He also had an excellent scout."

Dakota laughed.

"Hello, tinhorn," he said. "I wondered when you were going to get around to recognizing me. Are you still using the revolver you hit me with? I thought you probably bent the barrel on my hard head."

Wynne continued to ignore him. He said, "I told Elling I'd find you somewhere on the road and give you his offer. You don't have to take it, of course, but if you don't, you'd better go back to Custer City and start a business there. Elling has given orders for you to be shot on sight in Deadwood."

"Then, by God, he'll have to shoot me," Hargadine said. "I'm not selling out, and I'm not going back to Custer City."

"He won't be the one who'll shoot you," Wynne said irritably. "One of his hired gunslingers will do it. I keep telling you that. You can't get at Elling."

"Hargadine, he's been lying to you all the time," Dakota said. "It wasn't possible for Elling to leave Sidney when Wynne's wire said he did and beat you up here, not if he brought what he'd need to start a saloon and gambling hall. Wynne double-crossed you just like the twins and Abby have been telling you. Ask him how much Elling paid him."

"He got drunk on the way up here, didn't he?" Wynne asked. "I told you in Cheyenne that night he was not the man for the job."

"He got drunk at Fort Laramie," Hargadine admitted, "but I don't think that held us up any."

Dakota started toward Wynne, intending to settle this now, regardless of what Hargadine did or said. But before he could get his hands on Wynne, a commotion broke out from one side of the "joy wagon." Janie was screaming, and Abby was swearing, and then there was the solid whack of hand on flesh, and Janie screamed again.

The men wheeled toward the wagon. Dakota saw Abby holding a handful of Janie's hair in one hand while she drew the other hand back and slapped Janie again, rocking her head with the blow.

Hargadine shouted, "Abby, stop it!"

But Abby didn't stop. She hit Janie again and yelled angrily, "This little bitch has got something to tell you, and she's going to tell you, or I'll beat her to death."

Hargadine started toward Abby, but Jubal stepped in front of him.

"Let her alone, Sam."

Dakota kept his eyes on Wynne. He guessed that it was one development Wynne had not counted on. Suddenly nervous, Wynne began edging toward his horse.

When Abby reached Hargadine with the sobbing Janie, she said, "You're going to hear something me and the twins have guessed all the time, but I never knew for sure until I got it out of Janie a while ago. Like a damn fool, you got your head turned by a pretty face. Janie maneuvered you into bed with her, but before she let you have it, you told her about the gold and where you'd hid it. Now tell him what you did, Janie. Tell him, or I'll beat you until you won't know Monday from Sunday."

Everyone in the wagon train had heard the racket by this time. People came running toward the tent, but for Abby and Hargadine, the world beyond Janie did not exist.

"I told Jack Rawls," Janie whispered. "Rawls was working for Wynne, and he was working for Elling. That's how the outlaws knew where to find the gold—"

Wynne made a lunge toward his horse, but Dakota reached him before he got to the animal. He grabbed Wynne by the shoulder and hauled him back. His free hand plucked his knife from its scabbard. He brought the point up to Wynne's throat and pricked him deeply enough to draw blood.

"Jubal," he said, "would you like Wynne's ear for a watch fob? All you have to do is dry it in the sun for a while!"

"No!" Wynne screamed. "No! Sam, get this animal off of me!"

Hargadine was having trouble keeping up with everything that was happening. He said half-heartedly, "Don't do it, Jones."

Jubal tapped Dakota on the arm that held the knife.

"Let him talk, Dakota," he said mildly. "He's got something to say, and I want to hear it."

Dakota pressed the knife point a little harder into Wynne's throat.

"Like where Rawls is right now?"

"He's in Deadwood," Wynne whimpered.

"Go on."

"Elling's place is called Jake's Pleasure Castle. Rawls and Laird are both there. They expect Sam to arrive tomorrow, and they'll shoot him off his horse before he gets to Elling's place."

"Did he talk the Indians into jumping us?"

"Yes. He knew Big Bear. He told Big Bear the

train had lots of whisky and would be easy to take, because you didn't have good rifles or good men who would fight. He stayed close enough so that, if the Indians whipped you, he'd be able to get the gold after they left."

Dakota stepped back and slid his knife into the scabbard.

"What do you want done with this son of a bitch, Hargadine?"

"Let him go," Hargadine said. "You're riding south, Duke. I'm going into Deadwood, and I'm going to take Elling. If you ever show your face in this country again, I'll kill you."

Wynne staggered to his horse. He stepped into the saddle, then sat there a moment, tenderly feeling his throat. His hand came away red. He stared at it, then at Dakota. He put his horse into a run and did not look back.

Hargadine looked at Janie. She stood with her head down, her body shaking with sobs.

"I wonder what I ever saw in her," he said. "I don't want to see her again." He turned to Jubal. "I'm riding into Deadwood tonight. Want to go?"

"Sure," Jubal said.

"Me, too," Tubal said.

All three looked at Dakota, not saying anything, just waiting.

"I'll ride along," he said. "I'm real anxious to have a little visit with Jack Rawls."

"God help him," Abby said.

Chapter 24

Dakota ate supper with Barney Ryan and then saddled his sorrel. By that time, it was dark. He hesitated a moment, looking at the Nelson wagon and the small fire beside it. Nora was sitting there, her back to him. Bud wasn't in sight.

"You'd better see her before you leave," Ryan said.

Dakota turned toward Barney. He wasn't irritated at being pushed toward Nora as he had been in the past. He thought about that and wasn't sure why. He said, "Yeah, maybe I should."

Ryan held out his hand. "Good luck, Dakota. I can't say I approve of what you're doing. You hired out to get this wagon train to Deadwood. That didn't include risking your life in a gunfight just so Hargadine could start a saloon and gambling joint—but I understand why you're doing it."

Surprised, Dakota said, "You do?"

"Sure," Ryan said. "It's the way the good Lord made you. I don't think you're capable of staying here in camp while Hargadine and the Burke boys ride into town for a fight. You never turned your back on a fight in your life."

"It's a little more than that," Dakota said thoughtfully. "I want Rawls if he's in Deadwood, but there's still something else. Hargadine hired me because I had a reputation as a fighting man. That was what he wanted more than a scout. Maybe it wasn't exactly what I agreed to, but since it's what he hired me for, I'd better do it."

"Sure, sure. I still say that, if there's a fight around somewhere, you'll get into it." Barney Ryan smiled gently. "But after you get a family, maybe you'll change. Some men do."

Dakota walked to the Nelson wagon, leading his sorrel. He said, "Nora."

She rose slowly and faced him. She was pale, her hands fisted at her sides, and he realized she had been crying. She said in a low tone, "Be careful when you get to Deadwood. Maybe it's a waste of breath to tell you that, but I want you to come back. I'd try to argue you out of going, but you're a stubborn man. I know there isn't any use."

He stared at her in surprise. He had never thought of himself as a stubborn man. She was the stubborn one, stubborn and willful and . . . He dropped the reins and reached out and took her into his arms. He said, "This is the damnedest thing. You think I'm stubborn and willful and ornery but you were willing to go with me."

She nodded. "I still am."

"Well then, I guess I'd better take you," he said. "I figure we're going to have a—well, I guess you'd say we won't have a dull marriage."

She continued to look at him, saying nothing. Just waiting.

"I'm a little slow, Nora. It's going to take some time for you to make a civilized man out of a savage, but I'll try. I didn't know how I felt about you until just now. Seems like we've been fighting most of the time since we left Cheyenne, but, well, if we hadn't both felt so much, I guess we wouldn't have done any fighting. So there it is. Will you marry me?"

"Yes," she said.

"It'll be a tough life," he warned, "full of sweat and hard work and maybe danger. It won't be like running a millinery store in Deadwood."

"I'm used to sweat and hard work," she said, "and we've had some danger since we left Cheyenne. I can get used to that, too. If you remember, I told you I was going to start a millinery shop unless something better came along. It did."

"I hope so," he said gravely. "I know of a little valley in the Wind River country that would make a fine ranch, unless somebody has beaten us to it. It's a long way from civilization, and there's a lot of Indians around there—"

"I think you're hoorawing me," she said, "but I am not going to get mad. I have my temper under perfect control. Indians don't scare me one little bit. I refuse to let you bait me, Dakota Jones."

He pulled her to him and kissed her, and then Bud came around the end of the wagon.

"Mush," he said in disgust. "I never saw so much mush in my life. When I get a girl, there won't be any mush like that. I can tell something else, Dakota. Nora never has her temper under perfect control. And there's another thing you ought to know. She made up her mind a long time ago that she was going to marry you—"

"Bud," Dakota said amiably, "I let myself get trapped. And also, I expect you to come with us. We'll need a good cowboy to help start our ranch."

Bud blushed. "I'll be the best doggone cowboy you ever seen," he promised.

Dakota nodded, but he was looking at Nora.

"I've got to go," he said.

He kissed her again and got away fast.

When he reached the tent, he found Hargadine and the Burke boys waiting for him. They mounted, and the four of them rode away, Dakota and Hargadine in the lead, the Burkes following. Abby waved goodbye. Dakota and the twins waved back, but if Hargadine saw her, he ignored her gesture.

There was no moon, and the thin starshine left the bottom of the canyon in nearly total blackness. They rode slowly but steadily, no one saying anything until hours later when the lights of Deadwood came into view. The camp stretched along the bottom of a gulch, three miles long and fifty yards wide.

It was long after midnight, and most of the shacks they passed were dark. The business section lay ahead of them, but even here there were only a few lights, probably in the lobbies of the hotels or in some of the saloons that stayed open late.

"We'd better decide how we're going to play this," Dakota said.

"All right," Hargadine said. "The only thing I have to say is that Jake Elling's my meat. Tonight's the end of it for one of us."

"Rawls is mine," Dakota said. "As long as I live, I won't forget Dan Kraft and his wife and the baby they lost. Rawls wasn't there, but he was responsible."

"Tubal and me will go in first," Jubal said. "They may be locked up by now. If they are, I'll kick the door in. You come in last, Sam. I don't figure they'll be looking for you tonight, so maybe we'll surprise 'em.

"I think we will," Tubal said. "Duke Wynne was probably telling the truth on that."

"I'll give him that much credit," Dakota said. "I doubt that we would have got this far if we'd waited till tomorrow. Rawls and Laird and some of the rest of Elling's bunch would have smoked us down from the brush."

"Sam, you know Elling," Jubal said. "Where would you guess he'd be?"

"In his office," Hargadine said. "He's a great

one for playing the percentages. That's why he hires men like Rawls and Laird. They take the chances, not Elling." He paused, then added bitterly, "I should have believed you about Duke. Elling always seems to be able to buy men like him. I just couldn't accept the possibility that he would sell me out."

"All right," Dakota said. "I'll go in with the Burkes, Hargadine. We'll clear the way for you. Then it'll be your game."

"My game," Hargadine said tensely. "I've spent most of my life hating the bastard. It's been like a fire that burns like hell but never consumes me. I've got to get it over with."

Five minutes later, Jubal said, "There it is. On the left."

Chapter 25

The street was too dark to read the big sign above the door, but the letters, JAKE'S PLEASURE CASTLE, were printed on a window. The light inside was bright, so Dakota guessed Elling hadn't locked up yet. Still, they couldn't be sure until they tried the door. It was possible that the front door was locked, and the swampers were cleaning the place to get ready for the next day's business.

"Keep riding," Dakota said.

The street was empty except for a few drunks making their way home from some of the late-closing saloons. Dakota turned toward a hitch rail beyond Elling's place.

They dismounted and tied up, and then, with their guns in their hands, moved quickly back along the edge of the street. A man, probably a guard, came into the street from the alley. He turned to run, but before he could give the alarm, Dakota caught him and knocked him cold with a down-swinging blow of his gun barrel.

They reached the door of Elling's saloon. Dakota said softly, "Try it, Jubal."

Jubal put his hand on the knob and turned it gently.

"It ain't locked."

"Shove it open quick," Dakota said. "We're going in fast and spread out. They may be more ready for us than we're figuring."

For just a moment, Jubal hesitated, turning his head to look at Dakota. There was a short interval of time, the four men motionless in the near darkness, the tension that had gripped all of them from the instant they had ridden out of camp now strained to the breaking point.

This was the moment they had been waiting for during the long trip from Cheyenne, the moment of life and death for the four of them, the moment of the future for Sam Hargadine . . .

Jubal turned the knob and flung the door open. He went in fast and swung right. One step behind, Tubal went left. Dakota followed, diving into the big room and turning right after Jubal.

Within a matter of seconds from the time the door slammed open, Dakota had the answer to the one big question. Elling's men were not ready for them. Perhaps they had not expected this kind of entrance, or, more probably, they had not expected Hargadine to show up until the following day.

Several miners and businessmen sat at tables with drinks in front of them. They spilled out of their chairs and scurried out of range, some going out through windows and others lunging to safety through a back door.

The rest, Elling's crew, most of them gamblers, went for their guns.

Smoke and flame darted from the muzzles of their revolvers. Dakota heard bullets slap into the wall above him and beside him. He had no time to count the enemy, but there were six or eight at least. Dakota knocked one of them backward with his first shot. Another went down with Dakota's second bullet in his chest.

Bracket lamps glowed around the room, and overhead, the chandeliers glittered brightly. Dakota moved forward toward a door in the back wall, which he guessed opened into Elling's office. He knew that Tubal was down. He felt a bullet burn its path across his right knee. He stumbled but recovered his balance and kept his feet under him. He fired a third time, smashing the kneecap of a gambler who had suddenly thrown down his gun and was trying to get out through the back door. The tinhorn went down in a hard fall, screaming in agony.

Jubal and Hargadine moved with Dakota across the smoke-filled room, their guns throwing out tongues of flame. Dakota heard Jubal curse and guessed that he had been hit. The next second, the door he had been moving toward slammed open, and Jack Rawls charged out, a double-barreled shotgun in his hands. He never had a chance to use it. Dakota's bullet sliced through his neck, cutting his jugular vein. He spilled to the floor and died in a great spreading pool of blood.

The guns stopped as suddenly as they had started. Hargadine and Dakota strode past the dead and wounded men on the floor and into the room Rawls had left. The light here was as bright as it was in the saloon.

A man sat at a desk with an open ledger in front of him, an ugly man with an oversized head and tremendously large hands that were spread palm down on the desk in front of him. Thick-lensed glasses covered his pale, cruel eyes, giving him an owlish expression.

Hargadine paused ten feet in front of the desk and reloaded his revolver. He said, "It's been a long time, Jake."

Elling nodded. "A long time," he said tonelessly.

Elling looked at Dakota as if measuring him. Something was wrong, Dakota thought. Elling's men were supposed to stop Hargadine outside in the saloon if he came tonight, but they had failed. He was not a man to depend on them entirely, or on Rawls, who had stepped into the fight too late with his shotgun. Dakota was basing his judgment on what Hargadine had told him about Jake Elling. It was probably a correct estimate. Dakota knew he had better go on the assumption that it was.

Hargadine finished reloading his gun and

slipped it into the holster. He said, "Stand up, Jake. You can't draw sitting down. Only one of us is walking out of this room."

Elling smiled blandly and nodded. "I will agree with that. I expect it to be me." Still, he didn't move. He kept his gaze pinned on Dakota as he added, "You must be Dakota Jones. Rawls said you were a hard man to kill."

He leaned forward, his hands casually dropping off the top of the desk. Dakota made himself forget those hands for a split second. His gaze swept the room, fast. No one else in sight, but there was an opening to his left in the side wall. A closet. A thick red drape closed it off from the main office.

Dakota fired one shot into the closet, then grabbed the corner of the desk and yanked it toward him just as a sawed-off shotgun boomed from under the top of the desk. A charge of buckshot ripped into the opposite wall. If Dakota had not jerked the desk around to a sharp angle, Hargadine's legs would have been cut out from under him.

Elling was on his feet, right hand clawing for his Colt. Hargadine's gun was in his hand now. He fired twice; the bullets slammed Elling against the wall. He stayed propped upright for only a few seconds, long enough to whisper, "Rawls was right." He fell to the floor and rolled over on his face.

Dakota stepped to the closet and yanked the drape back. The skinny guard named Laird sat with his back to the wall, his head lolling forward on his chest. One hand was pressed against his belly, blood trickling between his fingers.

Picking up Laird's revolver, Dakota turned to Hargadine, who was staring at Elling's body.

"He never intended to give me an even break," Hargadine said. "Not when we came in or here at the last. That was one thing Duke said that was true."

Dakota reloaded his .45, then looked up to see Jubal standing in the doorway on one leg, his right hand clutching the casing. He said, "I got it when we were about halfway across the room. Tubal caught a slug along the ribs that knocked him down, but it just gouged out a chunk of meat. He'll be all right." He nodded at Dakota. "How about you?"

"Just a burn on my thigh," Dakota said. "It stings a little is all."

"I came through without a scratch," Hargadine said wonderingly. "I guess I'd better thank all three of you." He paused, nodded at Dakota, and added with an effort, "There's been a few times on the way up here that I hated you, Jones, and I wondered why in the hell I ever hired you. Now I know—you're a sort of buckskin genius. How'd you get onto that shotgun Elling was holding under his desk? And Laird back there in the closet?"

"Elling didn't act right for a man who liked the odds in his favor," Dakota said. "I didn't know he had the shotgun across his knees, but when I saw him pull his hands off the top of the desk and lean forward, I figured he wasn't running any chances."

Now that the shooting was over, several men came into the room. One was the marshal, who glanced around and said, "Looks like a slaughter-house in here." Another was a doctor, who carried a black bag and said he always came on the run when he heard shooting, night or day. The third one was a fat man, who said he owned the building and would Hargadine want to pick up Elling's lease? Hargadine would.

Dakota gripped Hargadine's arm. "I'm going back to camp, and I'll have the wagons here by the middle of the afternoon. You staying with the Burke boys?"

Hargadine nodded. "I'll see they're taken care of." He wiped his sweaty face with a handkerchief, and then he said something that surprised Dakota. "As soon as you get to camp, tell Abby I'm all right."

"I'll tell her," Dakota said.

He went into the street, stepped into the saddle, and rode out of town. He would be back soon enough with Nora to find a preacher and get married. And then with a thousand dollars in pocket, they would ride out of Deadwood, him and Nora and Bud.

They would find their future somewhere west of the Black Hills, maybe in the Wind River country. And it wouldn't be dull.

About the Author

Wayne D. Overholser won three Spur Awards from the Western Writers of America and has a long list of fine Western titles to his credit. He was born in Pomeroy, Washington, and attended the University of Montana, University of Oregon, and the University of Southern California before becoming a public schoolteacher and principal in various Oregon communities. He began writing for Western pulp magazines in 1936 and, within a couple of years, was a regular contributor to Street & Smith's *Western Story Magazine* and Fiction House's *Lariat Story Magazine*. *Buckaroo's Code* (1947) was his first Western novel and remains one of his best. In the 1950s and 1960s, having retired from academic work to concentrate on writing, he would publish as many as four books a year under his own name or a pseudonym, most prominently as Joseph Wayne.

His Western novels are based on a solid knowledge of the history and customs of the 19th-Century West, particularly when set in his two favorite Western states, Oregon and Colorado. Many of his novels are first-person narratives, a technique that tends to bring an added dimension of vividness to the frontier experiences of his narrators, and frequently, the female characters one encounters in his stories are among the most memorable. He wrote his numerous novels with a consistent skill and an uncommon sensitivity to the depths of human character. Almost invariably, Overholser's stories weave a spell of their own with their scenes and images of social and economic forces often in conflict, and the diverse ways of life and personalities that made the American Western frontier such a unique time and place in human history.

Center Point Large Print
600 Brooks Road / PO Box 1
Thorndike, ME 04986-0001 USA

(207) 568-3717

US & Canada:
1 800 929-9108
www.centerpointlargeprint.com